The
FANTASTIC SECRET
of OWEN JESTER

Also by Barbara O'Connor

Beethoven in Paradise
Me and Rupert Goody
Moonpie and Ivy
Fame and Glory in Freedom, Georgia
Taking Care of Moses
How to Steal a Dog
Greetings from Nowhere
The Small Adventure of Popeye and Elvis

THE FANTASTIC SECRET of OWEN JESTER

by **Barbara O'Connor**

SQUARE
FISH

FARRAR STRAUS GIROUX
NEW YORK

Special thanks to Ron Leonard, Vice-President of International VentureCraft Corporation, the maker of SportSubs, for his expert advice and information about those amazing little submarines. Viola couldn't have done it better.

SQUARE FISH

An Imprint of Macmillan

Library of Congress Cataloging-in-Publication Data
O'Connor, Barbara.
    The fantastic secret of Owen Jester / Barbara O'Connor.
        p.   cm.
    Summary: After Owen captures an enormous bullfrog, names it Tooley
Graham, then has to release it, he and two friends try to use a small submarine that
fell from a passing train to search for Tooley in the Carter, Georgia, pond it came
from, while avoiding nosy neighbor Viola.
    ISBN 978-0-312-67430-4
    [1. Adventure and adventurers—Fiction.   2. Submersibles—Fiction.
3. Bullfrog—Fiction.   4. Frogs—Fiction.   5. Family life—Georgia—Fiction.
6. Georgia—Fiction.]   I. Title.

PZ7.O217Fan 2010
[Fic]—dc22
                                                                2009019249

Originally published in the United States by Farrar Straus Giroux
First Square Fish Edition: October 2011
Square Fish logo designed by Filomena Tuosto
Book designed by Natalie Zanecchia
mackids.com

5   7   9   10   8   6   4

AR: 4.7 / LEXILE: 770L

For Leslie
My friend
Who knows all my fantastic secrets

The
FANTASTIC SECRET
of OWEN JESTER

CHAPTER
ONE

Owen Jester tiptoed across the gleaming linoleum floor and slipped the frog into the soup.

It swam gracefully under the potatoes, pushing its froggy legs through the pale yellow broth. It circled the carrots and bumped into the celery and finally settled beside a parsnip, its bulging eyes staring unblinkingly up at Owen.

"See, Tooley? I told you," Owen said. "It's not hot."

He plucked a carrot out of the soup and popped it into his mouth.

Still cold.

Not yet heated up for his grandfather's supper.

Owen scurried into the pantry and hunkered down on the floor among the sacks of potatoes and jars of pickled okra and waited for Earlene.

3

When he heard the *clomp, clomp* of her heavy black shoes on the wooden stairs, he slapped a hand over his mouth to stifle a giggle. When he heard the kitchen door swing open, he slapped his other hand over his mouth, his shoulders shaking with a silent laugh. Then he peeked through the crack in the pantry door.

Earlene stomped over to the stove in that no-nonsense way of hers. She picked up a wooden spoon from the kitchen counter and peered into the pot. Then she placed the spoon back on the counter, stepped away from the stove, jammed both fists into her waist, and said, "Owen."

Her voice had that sharp edge to it that Owen had heard so many times before. He ducked back against the pantry wall and held his breath.

And then, quick as lightning, the pantry door burst open and Earlene's hand shot in, grabbed Owen by the collar, and yanked him to his feet.

Earlene was not a yeller.

Earlene was a snapper.

"Get that frog out of there," she snapped.

"You think that's funny?" she snapped.

She gave his collar a shake.

"You are a bad, bad child," she snapped. "And I thank my lucky stars every day that you are not mine."

She gave his collar another shake. "And I thank the good Lord up above that your grandfather doesn't know what's going on in this house."

She stomped over to the counter and began arranging pill bottles on a tray. "The very idea of that poor sick old man up there in the bed not able to do a thing but sleep and eat applesauce and you down here thinking up ways to make my life miserable."

Earlene sure knew how to ruin a good time.

After supper, Owen sat on his closet floor beside the plastic tub where Tooley lived and looked down at the frog. Tooley was the biggest, greenest, slimiest, most beautiful bullfrog ever to be seen in Carter, Georgia.

It had taken Owen nearly a month to catch him. A month of clomping through mud and scooping with fishnets and buckets and colanders and even a hamster cage. A month of squatting on logs, holding his breath, not moving a muscle, watching that big frog with the heart-shaped red spot between his bulging yellow eyes. A month of telling his friends Travis and Stumpy he was going to catch that frog no matter what.

And then one day, just last week, he did.

The right scoop with the right net at the right time.

He had brought the frog home and made him a perfect frog house in a plastic tub in the closet.

And he had named him Tooley Graham.

Tooley after his cousin who lived in Alabama and played in a rock-and-roll band and wore leather bracelets and made everyone mad when he came to Georgia to visit the family at Thanksgiving. (Everyone but Owen, who thought Tooley was cool.)

And Graham after the big pond where the bullfrog had lived before Owen caught him. Graham Pond.

Owen poked the frog with his finger. "Come on, Tooley," he said. "You gotta eat *something*."

But Tooley wouldn't even look at the dead fly that Owen had dropped into the water in the tub.

So Owen laid the chicken wire back on top of the tub, put a brick on top of the chicken wire, and flopped onto his bed, staring up at the ceiling. Travis and Stumpy were probably skateboarding over at the Bi-Lo parking lot. Maybe they were throwing rocks at the Quaker State Oil sign out on Highway 11. Or maybe they were thinking up some great new way to torture their dreaded enemy, Viola.

But Owen was stuck here in his bedroom, thanks to Earlene, who had tattled on him big-time as soon as his mother had gotten home from work. He could tell his mother had thought that soup trick was at least a little bit funny. He had seen the corners of her mouth twitch when Earlene went on and on about what a bad, bad boy he was.

But his mother had told his father and his father had slammed his fist on the kitchen table and hollered at Owen and now here he was in his bedroom, just him and Tooley.

Owen wished they had never moved in with his grandfather. He wished they still lived in that little house over on Tupelo Road. Travis had lived next door and Stumpy had lived across the street and life had been good.

But then the hardware store had closed and his father didn't have a job, so they had moved across town to live with his grandfather.

There were three good things and three bad things about living with his grandfather.

The three good things were:

1. There was a lot of land around the house, with woods and paths and sheds and the big pond where Tooley had lived.
2. There was a falling-down barn behind

the house that was filled with stuff, like a rusty unicycle and a crate full of horse-shoes and about a hundred rolls of chicken wire.

3. Train tracks ran behind the woods below the house, and every few days the whistle blew late at night as the train roared through Carter.

The three bad things were:

1. Earlene had been working for his grandfather for as long as Owen had been alive. Maybe longer. Earlene was grumpy and needed everything to be clean.

2. Travis and Stumpy lived farther away and sometimes did things without him.

3. Viola lived next door.

Owen did not like Viola.

There were a lot of reasons why he did not like Viola, but the first four were:

1. Viola was nosy.

2. Viola was bossy.

3. Viola wore glasses that made her eyes look big, like a fly's.

4. Viola was a know-it-all.

There was only one good thing about Viola:

She had allergies.

Viola was allergic to pine and grass and dust and dogs and just about every good thing in life.

This was a good thing because it meant that Viola didn't like to play in the woods or the fields or down by the pond. And she never went inside Owen's grandfather's house, where Owen's dogs, Pete and Leroy, left tumbleweeds of fur along the baseboards of every room.

Owen checked on Tooley one more time before he turned off the lamp beside the bed. Then he sat by the window and took a deep breath of the summer night air. It smelled like pine and grass and honeysuckle.

Far off in the distance, the train whistle blew. Owen waited, listening for the faint clatter of the train on the tracks to get louder and louder as it got closer to Carter.

In a blink, the train was whooshing down the tracks behind the house.

Clatter, clatter, clatter.

And then . . . something else.

A noise Owen had never heard before.

From way down by the tracks.

A thud.

The crack of wood.

A tumble, tumble, tumble sound.

Then the *clatter, clatter, clatter* of the train grew fainter and fainter until the only sound left was the chirp of the crickets in the garden beneath the window.

TWO

H e's sad."

"He is not."

"He is, too."

"He is *not*." Owen stamped his foot and glared at Viola. He reached into the cardboard box and nudged the grasshopper closer to Tooley.

The frog didn't move.

"Besides," Viola said, "frogs only eat bugs that are alive." She stepped closer to Owen. "Everyone knows that," she added.

Owen quickly stepped aside before Viola's pudgy white arm could touch him. "Your mother's calling you," he said.

Viola reached into the box and stroked Tooley's back with one finger. "You should let him go," she said.

Well, that just proved what Owen had known all along. Viola was dumb.

"You're dumb," Owen said. "What kind of person would go to all that trouble to catch the best frog in Carter, Georgia, and then turn around and let it go?"

"A *nice* person," Viola said. "A good person. A kind person. A—"

"Your mother's calling you," Owen said again.

"You're mean, Owen." Viola tossed her stringy hair over her shoulder, adjusted her glasses, wiped grass off the back of her shorts, and stalked off to the hedge that separated her backyard from Owen's grandfather's. Then, just before disappearing through the opening at the bottom of the hedge, she turned around and added, "And that frog is sad."

Owen scooped Tooley up and held him close to his face.

"You're not sad, are you, fella?" he said. He examined the frog. His shiny skin. His yellow throat. His froggy toes.

Owen glanced over at the hedge to make sure Viola was gone, then whispered to Tooley, "You want a *live* bug?"

Tooley wiggled a little bit and placed a webbed foot on Owen's cheek.

"Me and Travis and Stumpy will find you some big ole juicy ones," Owen said. Then he took Tooley over to the back porch and placed him in the outside frog house, a plastic tub under the stairs. The outside frog house was just like the inside frog house, only bigger, so Tooley had more room to swim. Owen had put a log in the tub for Tooley to sit on and added some magnolia leaves that floated on the water like lily pads.

On his way over to Tupelo Road, Owen worried about Tooley.

He wouldn't eat.

He didn't jump like he had at first.

He didn't swim like he had at first.

His eyes didn't seem quite as shiny and his skin didn't seem quite as smooth.

But mixed in with the worry about Tooley was some thinking.

Owen kept thinking about that noise he had heard last night.

That thud.

That crack of wood.

That tumble, tumble, tumble sound.

Something had fallen off the train.

Owen was sure of it.

He had planned to dash down to the tracks first thing this morning and look for it.

But then Viola had crawled through the opening in the hedge and stuck her nosy nose into his business and said all that stuff about Tooley being sad and now he had to find some live bugs. But he couldn't stop thinking about that noise or wondering if he was right about something falling off the train.

And if something *had* fallen off the train, what in the world could it be?

THREE

"How much do bullfrogs eat?" Travis said.

Owen cupped his hands over the cricket. "Got him!"

He dropped the cricket into the jar. "That's five," he said. "That should be enough."

"What about this?" Stumpy held up a fat, muddy worm.

"Nah," Owen said. "I don't think frogs eat worms."

Stumpy tossed the worm into the flower bed and wiped his hand on his shorts.

"Maybe we could build a cage for Tooley," Travis said. He took his baseball cap off, swished it around in the water in the birdbath, and put it back on. Dirty water ran down the side of his face and dripped onto his shirt.

"Y'all get out of my garden!" Joleen Berkus hollered out the window.

The boys ran through the garden, trampling marigolds and tripping on cantaloupe vines, until they reached Stumpy's yard.

Joleen Berkus had moved into the house where Owen used to live. She had torn down Owen's fort and made a garden. She had hauled off all the car parts on the back porch and put a rocking chair there. She had painted right over JESTER on the mailbox and stenciled on BERKUS in perfect black letters, and now she spent the livelong day hollering at Owen and Travis and Stumpy every time they set foot in her yard (which used to be Owen's).

"Maybe we could build a cage," Travis repeated as they flopped down on Stumpy's front steps to examine the crickets.

"What kind of cage?" Owen said.

"A cage in the pond." Travis tapped on the side of the cricket jar.

A cage in the pond?

Hmmmmm.

That wasn't a half-bad idea!

"We could use that chicken wire in the barn," Owen said.

"Yeah!" Stumpy said. "Bugs and stuff could get right through it."

"And we could make a door so we could take him out," Owen said.

And so the boys planned.

They planned how big the cage would be and where they would put it and where they would get the things they would need to build it.

All afternoon they planned.

And the more they planned, the better Owen felt about Tooley.

Owen had been so busy planning, he had forgotten about the noise.

The thud.

The crack of wood.

The tumble, tumble, tumble sound.

But that evening at the supper table, he remembered.

"I'm going outside," he said, pushing his chair back with a scrape and heading for the door.

His father didn't even look up from his pork chop.

His mother said, "Be back before dark."

Earlene squinted over at him from the sink and muttered something under her breath about bad manners and green beans.

The two dogs, Pete and Leroy, leaped off the porch after Owen, and the three of them raced across the yard, into the woods, and along the path toward the train tracks.

Owen had explored every inch of the woods and fields around his grandfather's house. The main path zigzagged around trees and boulders to the middle of the woods. Then it forked. The path to the left led to a field full of weeds and pricker bushes, then continued on down to a tilted, rotting dock at Graham Pond.

The path to the right led around the pond to the train tracks on the other side.

Owen was not allowed to go down to the train tracks.

Travis and Stumpy were not allowed to go down to the train tracks.

Owen and Travis and Stumpy went down to the train tracks nearly every day.

They had put about a million dollars' worth of pennies on the tracks for the train to flatten (and a few nickels and quarters, too).

One time Stumpy had put a liverwurst sandwich on the tracks, and when they went back the next day, not a crumb was left.

They had walked right up the middle of the tracks all the way to the main road and back again.

They had put their ears against the metal rail to listen for the train.

But the train only came late at night.

"Come on, boys," Owen called to Pete and Leroy when he got to the end of the path at the tracks.

The two dogs trotted along behind him, sniffing at every tree and rock and pricker bush.

Owen looked up the tracks.

Then he looked down the tracks.

Nothing unusual.

Just the same stuff he saw nearly every day.

The mound of red dirt that ran beside the tracks.

Gravel.

Weeds.

A few rusty soda cans.

A broken bottle.

Nothing unusual.

"Shoot," Owen said out loud, making Pete and Leroy look at him and cock their heads.

Owen had wanted to find whatever it was that had fallen off the train all by himself. But maybe he should tell Travis and Stumpy.

Owen and Travis and Stumpy had always been good at finding stuff together.

But then there was the problem of nosy Viola, lurking around, following them, spying on them.

He would have to wait until just the right time to tell Travis and Stumpy.

"Come on, boys," Owen called again to Pete and Leroy.

Then he headed back up the path toward home, with the two dogs trotting along behind him.

CHAPTER
FOUR

Shhh." Owen pressed a finger to his lips and motioned for Travis and Stumpy to duck behind the barn door.

He peeked through a crack in the warped boards.

Viola was tromping across the yard, swinging a Girl Scout canteen with one hand and pushing at her glasses with the other.

"Dang," Owen whispered. "She's coming this way."

Travis jabbed a finger up toward the hayloft.

Owen nodded.

The three boys dashed across the dirt floor of the barn and scurried up the rickety ladder to the loft. They flopped down on their stomachs, their cheeks pressed against the hay-covered floor, and waited.

"I know y'all are in there, Owen." Viola's irritating voice drifted into the barn.

Travis poked Owen with an elbow and Stumpy made a little snort noise. Owen flapped a hand at both of them and mouthed, "Be quiet."

Viola's sandals made a slapping noise as she entered the barn and stopped at the bottom of the ladder.

"I know y'all are in here." That irritating voice slithered up the ladder and circled around Owen.

Dang! That girl sure was annoying.

"What are y'all doing?" The voice pounded Owen on the back of the head.

The slapping sandals moved away from the ladder and shuffled over to the corner of the barn.

"What're y'all building?"

Owen lifted his head the teeny tiniest bit and peered over the edge of the loft. Viola was rummaging through the stuff that he and Travis and Stumpy had spent all morning gathering. Rolls of chicken wire. Tomato stakes. Baling wire. Twine. Old door hinges.

Viola poked at a roll of chicken wire. "I know what y'all are building," she said.

Travis pursed his lips and glared down at Viola.

Stumpy's eyes grew big and round as he looked at Owen in a *What now?* kind of way.

Owen crawled to the rear of the loft until he got to

a milk crate full of old tractor parts. He grabbed a greasy rubber fan belt, a handful of rusty nuts and bolts, and a broken gauge of some sort. Then he crawled back to the edge of the loft and began flinging the things down to the barn floor, trying to get as close to Viola as possible without actually hitting her.

The bolts made pingy noises as they hit garden tools and engine parts and ricocheted off the wheelbarrow and the lawn mower. The gauge skidded over the dirt floor and hit the wall of the barn with a crash, followed by the tinkle of broken glass.

The fan belt landed right on Viola's sandal. She jerked her foot away and gazed coolly up at Owen.

"Y'all are building something for that sad old frog," she said, giving her glasses a nudge up the bridge of her nose with her thumb.

"His name is Tooley and he's not sad," Owen called down from the loft.

Viola picked up the fan belt and twirled it around her finger. "Frogs don't have names."

"Says who?" Travis hollered down at Viola.

Stumpy pushed some hay off the edge of the loft. "Yeah, says who?" he said.

Viola brushed hay out of her hair and glared up at

the boys. "Says me and anyone else on the planet with half a brain." She tossed the fan belt onto the pile of chicken wire. "Frogs don't have names and don't want names. Frogs want to be frogs and live where frogs are supposed to live."

"Oh, yeah?" Travis said.

"Oh, yeah?" Stumpy said.

"Your mother's calling you," Owen said.

As soon as the words left his mouth, Owen's stomach clenched up into a ball of angry. Why did he have to go and say that again?

First of all, he said it all the time.

Second of all, Viola never even blinked an eye when he said it, so what was the point?

And third of all, Viola's mother never called her. Viola's mother never did anything but sit on the porch in her bathrobe looking at magazines. The only time Owen had ever seen Viola's mother step one foot off her porch was the time she went to the flea market and came back with a bunch of tiki torches. Viola had told him the tiki torches were for a Hawaiian luau party. Owen had peeked through the hedge every day for nearly a week to see the Hawaiian luau party, but all he ever saw was a pile of tiki torches and a barbecue grill full of rainwater.

Viola pushed aside the tomato stakes with the toe of her sandal. She inspected a tangled roll of baling wire. She squinted through her thick glasses at the rusty door hinges.

"Y'all are building a cage," she said.

Owen hurried down the ladder and grabbed the door hinges from her. He jammed them into his pocket and said, "Go away."

"Yeah, go away." Travis jumped off the last rung of the ladder and stood between Viola and the pile of stuff, his feet spread, his arms folded, his chin stuck out.

Stumpy jumped from halfway down the ladder and landed on the barn floor with an *oomph*.

"You don't really need hinges, you know." Viola nodded toward the baling wire. "And staples would work better than that wire."

"Staples are for paper, you ninny," Travis said.

"Yeah," Stumpy said. "Staples are for paper, you ninny."

But Owen stayed quiet. He was trying to keep his irritation from getting the best of him and turning him into a foot-stomping baby.

But it was hard.

Because he knew Viola was right about the staples.

And he knew she didn't mean staples like the little ones for paper. She meant those heavy-duty kind like his father used to staple plastic over the windows in the winter at their old house on Tupelo Road.

"I know where there's a staple gun," Viola said, grabbing her canteen off the hay bale.

She turned to Owen and looked smug.

Owen hated it when Viola looked smug.

More than anything, he wanted to say "Where?"

But he knew that Viola wanted him to say "Where?"

Which was why she was looking so smug.

So instead of saying "Where?" Owen said, "Rocket."

Rocket was the secret code word that he and Travis and Stumpy had made up to ditch Viola. They had agreed that if one of them said "Rocket," they would all run as fast as they could to their hiding place down by the train tracks.

So that's what they did.

They ran as fast as they could out of the barn, across the yard, down the path, through the woods, and around the pond. They crossed to the other side of the tracks, pushed their way through the scrubby bushes, and crawled up under the branches of an enormous rotten oak tree that had fallen years ago and landed against a pine tree, forming a perfect tepee.

The boys were gasping and laughing and high-fiving each other when Pete and Leroy came sniffing through the brush, tails wagging, noses sniffing.

"Uh-oh," Owen said. "I hope Viola didn't follow them."

Owen crawled out of the tree tepee and looked around.

No sign of Viola.

Good, he thought.

Then the time had come.

He was going to tell Travis and Stumpy about the thing that had fallen off the train.

CHAPTER
FIVE

The boys looked all afternoon. They combed the woods. They tromped through pricker bushes. They waded along the edges of the pond, their feet sinking in the gooey mud.

They found a plastic milk crate with the bottom broken out.

They found a coffee can full of mud.

They found a piece of PVC pipe with PROPERTY OF MONROE COUNTY stamped on the side.

And they found an old metal thing with a rusty bolt sticking out of it.

But none of those things seemed like something that would have fallen off the train and made the noise that Owen heard.

The thud.

The crack of wood.

The tumble, tumble, tumble sound.

"Are you sure the noise came from around here?" Travis said, tossing a handful of rocks into the pond.

"Sure, I'm sure," Owen said.

"I mean, maybe it was farther up that way." Travis nodded up the tracks. "Maybe it wasn't near the pond."

Owen shrugged. "Maybe."

"Then you know what that means," Stumpy said.

Owen and Travis looked at Stumpy and waited.

"That means it could be up yonder behind Viola's house." Stumpy set his mouth in a hard line and drew his eyebrows together.

A deep, dead, gloomy silence fell over them.

They stared at their shoes, their hands shoved in their pockets.

Suddenly Owen's head shot up and he snapped his fingers. "Allergies!" he hollered, grinning.

Travis and Stumpy stared at Owen.

"Viola never goes back that far," Owen said. "There's weeds and stuff back there. She hates that. She sneezes and gets sick and all." He shook his head. "Naw, Viola won't be nosing around here."

Owen looked up the tracks. He knew every inch of

them, how they curved slightly just beyond the pond, then continued on through the fields way in the back of Viola's house. After that they went over the main highway, out of Carter and into Fort Valley.

Out of Fort Valley and into Byron.

Out of Byron and into Macon.

And on and on, clear on through the state of Georgia.

As the sun sank lower and the sky grew darker, the boys agreed to come back to the tracks and look some more, if they could ditch that nosy Viola.

Then they headed back toward Owen's house to catch mosquitoes for Tooley.

"Here you go, Tooley," Owen said. "These are yummy." He opened the peanut butter jar and released three mosquitoes into the frog house in the closet. Then he spread a piece of newspaper over the top of the plastic tub to keep the mosquitoes from escaping.

He waited.

He listened, hoping to hear Tooley hopping around inside, catching the mosquitoes.

But it was quiet.

Owen lifted the corner of the newspaper and peeked inside. Tooley sat on the branch. The mosquitoes flitted around the plastic tub. One of them landed on the branch right beside Tooley, but the big green frog didn't move.

Not even one little bit.

Owen sighed.

He reached into the tub and lifted the bullfrog out. He examined Tooley's yellow throat, his webbed feet, his froggy face with the heart-shaped red spot between his eyes.

Owen got an icky feeling in the pit of his stomach.

Tooley *did* look a little sad.

Owen set the frog down on the floor beside his bed.

He waited.

Tooley didn't jump.

Owen nudged him a little.

Tooley didn't jump.

The first time Owen had set Tooley down on his bedroom floor, the frog had jumped clear across the room in one giant leap.

Owen sighed again.

He scooped Tooley up and put him back on the

branch in the frog house. He covered the frog house with the chicken wire and the brick, then went over to look out the window.

The moon cast a soft glow on the yard and the woods out back. The night was quiet for a few minutes, and then the faint clatter of the train drifted into the silence.

Louder, louder, louder.

Clatter, clatter, clatter.

The train roared by . . .

. . . and then was gone.

But this time, there was no thud.

No crack of wood.

No tumble, tumble, tumble sound.

Owen tried to imagine something in the bushes or the gully or the woods somewhere out there beside the tracks.

Something that had fallen off the train.

But what?

What had fallen off the train?

And where was it?

Owen was determined to find it.

But first, he and Travis and Stumpy were going to have to build that cage for Tooley. It would be the best frog cage ever. It would be big enough for swimming and jumping. Half of it would be out of the water, with logs and leaves and squishy mud to sit in. The other half would be in the water, with room for Tooley to swim in big, big circles, kicking his froggy legs the livelong day. And a whole parade of water bugs and grasshoppers and crickets and flies would go right through the chicken-wire sides of the cage and Tooley would gobble them up.

And Tooley would not be sad.

CHAPTER
SIX

Owen tucked the duct tape under his T-shirt, motioned for Pete and Leroy, and tried to open the screen door so it wouldn't squeak.

He failed.

The screen door squeaked and Earlene's harsh voice thundered from the front hallway.

"Where are you going?"

"Out yonder," Owen called back.

Earlene stormed into the kitchen, wiping her hands on her apron and shaking her ugly ole head. "You're going nowhere till you sweep up every crumb of dirt and blade of grass you tracked in here last night. I don't know why on God's green earth you can't take your shoes off like I've told you a million times and . . ."

She yammered on and on but all Owen heard was *blah, blah, blah.*

He let out a big, heaving sigh and trudged to the broom closet.

"What's that under your shirt?" Earlene said, squinting over at him.

"Nothing."

The duct tape fell out from under his shirt and rolled across the kitchen floor. Earlene snatched it up and shook it at Owen. "What're you doing with this?"

"Nothing."

Earlene's face turned red as fire as she shoved the duct tape back into the junk drawer.

The whole time he was sweeping up dirt and grass, Earlene stood stiffly beside him, her fists jammed into her waist and the toe of her clunky shoe tap, tap, tapping on the floor while she yammered some more. Her voice swirled around the room like a horde of angry bees. Owen hummed to himself, very, very quietly so Earlene wouldn't hear. His humming helped turn Earlene's words into a steady buzz. But every now and then, a word tumbled out of the swirling buzz.

Frog.

Mud.

Disgusting.

Trouble.

Noise.

Owen hummed a little louder so he could shut out *all* of Earlene's words and think.

He thought about meeting Travis and Stumpy out in the barn. He thought about putting all the chicken wire and tomato stakes and stuff into the wheelbarrow and taking it down to the pond. He thought about how to keep Viola from sticking her nosy nose into his business and ruining all his fun.

"Hurry up," Owen called over his shoulder as he scurried down the path toward the pond, the hinges and baling wire banging and clanking as they bounced in the bottom of the wheelbarrow.

Travis and Stumpy huffed and puffed behind him, dragging a roll of chicken wire that left a trail in the pine needles scattered along the path.

When they got to the pond, they stopped, panting, wiping sweat off their brows.

"I was thinking we should attach the cage to the dock," Owen said. "That way, we can reach it without getting in the water."

Travis and Stumpy nodded in agreement.

So the boys dumped the stuff in the weeds beside the dock and set to work building a cage for Tooley.

But they didn't have wire cutters to cut the wire.

They didn't have a saw to cut the tomato stakes.

They didn't have a plan.

"We need a plan," Owen said.

"Yeah," Travis said.

"Yeah," Stumpy said.

Owen tossed the hinges into the wheelbarrow. "Let's hide this stuff in the bushes and go to Stumpy's and make a plan," he said.

While Joleen Berkus glared over at them from her glider on the porch, Owen and Travis and Stumpy sat on the sidewalk in front of Stumpy's house and made a plan for the frog cage on notebook paper.

First they made a list of the tools they would need, like wire cutters and a staple gun and a saw.

Then they drew a picture of the cage, showing the measurements for each of the sides and where the door would go.

They drew and wrote and drew and wrote and then . . .

. . . a short, fat shadow fell across the paper.

The boys looked up.

Viola stared down at them with her big fly-eyes through her thick glasses. "I know what you're doing," she said.

Owen looked back down at the notebook paper and pretended like he didn't see her chubby white legs standing there beside him.

"Jarvis has a staple gun," Viola said.

"Jarvis is a wormy-headed doofus," Travis said.

Stumpy slapped his knee and snorted.

Jarvis was Viola's brother, who sometimes went to high school and sometimes worked in a sign-painting shop over in Fort Valley.

He was pale and freckly and wore thick glasses that gave him fly-eyes, like Viola's.

"You shouldn't use hinges," Viola said. "They'll get too rusty."

"Do you hear somebody talking?" Travis said to Owen.

"I don't hear a thing," Owen said. "How about you, Stumpy?"

"Not one dang little thing," Stumpy said.

"Me neither," Travis said. "Not even a bossy toad-brain who thinks she knows everything there is to know about everything on the planet."

The boys huddled over the drawings on the notebook paper on the sidewalk and didn't look up.

Owen pretended like he wasn't irritated as all get-out at Viola. And he pretended like it hadn't suddenly occurred to him that Viola was right. Using hinges *wasn't* a very good idea. Maybe it would be better to use the baling wire to attach the top of the cage so it could be opened and closed.

He gathered up the papers and motioned for Travis and Stumpy to follow him.

The three boys trotted off toward Owen's grandfather's house, leaving Viola behind.

The boys worked on the frog cage down by the pond all afternoon. Every now and then, Owen ran up to the house to check on Tooley, who sat motionless in the frog house under the back stairs. Every time Owen checked, Tooley was sitting in the same spot, on top of a soggy magnolia leaf.

Every time, Owen poked him with a finger.

Every time, Tooley blinked one long, slow blink, but didn't move.

Owen tried to nudge Tooley so he would swim around the tub like he used to.

But Tooley wouldn't swim.

So Owen raced back down to the pond to work on the cage some more.

If they could finish the cage today, they could put it in the water and Tooley could move right in and be happy.

And then . . .

. . . first thing tomorrow morning, he could meet Travis and Stumpy down by the tracks and they could look for the thing that had fallen off the train.

CHAPTER
SEVEN

Owen stepped back and admired the cage.

It was perfect.

The boys had rolled out a piece of chicken wire and bent it into a large rectangle shape. Then they used the wire cutters that Travis had taken from his father's toolbox to cut two pieces of chicken wire, for the top and bottom of the cage. Since they didn't have a staple gun (and no way were they going to borrow one from Viola's fly-eyed brother, Jarvis), they used baling wire to attach a tomato stake to each of the four corners.

Next, they attached the bottom securely all around the edges. They attached the top loosely on one end so that they could lift it up and down, open and closed. They made a latch out of bent wire to hold the top closed.

They tested it a few times, opening and closing the top. Hooking and unhooking the latch.

Owen had never seen a finer cage.

Tooley was going to love it.

"Tooley's going to love it," Owen said.

Travis and Stumpy nodded.

"Now all we have to do is put it in the water," Owen said, and walked out onto the rickety dock and inspected the pond. He squinted into the murky water. "I wonder how deep it is here," he said.

Stumpy tossed a rock into the pond.

Ploink.

It disappeared out of sight.

Owen pulled a tomato stake out of the wheelbarrow. He walked to the edge of the dock and put the stake into the water until he felt the squishy mud on the bottom of the pond. He inched along the edge of the dock, poking the stake into the water until he could no longer feel the bottom.

"This is where it starts getting deeper," he said. "We should put the cage here."

He poked the stick into the pond some more, stirring up the muddy bottom. "One end can be in the shallow part so Tooley can get out of the water and one end can be in the deeper part so he can swim around."

So the boys sat on the dock and planned how they would position the cage in the pond. They debated which side of the dock was best and how deep the cage should be in the water and whether or not they should attach it to the dock with wire.

But before they could start carrying out their plans, a voice interrupted the still summer air.

A dreaded voice.

Viola's voice.

"O-o-o-o-o-o-wen!"

Owen looked at Travis and Travis looked at Stumpy and Stumpy looked at Owen.

"Dang!" Owen said.

"What's *she* want?" Travis said.

"Let's hide!" Stumpy said.

"O-o-o-o-o-o-wen!" Viola's voice drifted through the trees from up at Owen's house.

"We better get up there and see what she wants or she's liable to come down here," Owen said.

"Nah," Travis said. "She hates it here."

But Owen wasn't taking any chances. "Let's go," he said.

The boys raced up the path through the woods. When they got to Owen's backyard, Viola was sitting under the stairs beside the frog house.

"What are *you* doing here?" Owen said.

"Earlene's looking for you." She pushed at her glasses and peered into the plastic tub beside her. "Your frog looks terrible," she said.

"Go away," Owen said.

"Yeah, go away," Travis said.

Stumpy kicked at the dry red dirt of the yard, sending dust and pebbles in Viola's direction.

Viola stood up and wiped dirt off her shorts. "Is that water from the pond?" she said, pointing at the tub where Tooley sat, his big yellow eyes staring up out of the dirty water.

Owen pushed his irritation down, down, down, trying hard not to let it come busting out like it wanted to. "Why is Earlene looking for me?" he said.

"You should put water from the pond in there." Viola brushed past the boys and skipped toward the hedge. Then she turned around and said, "Earlene knows you took the wheelbarrow out of the barn and you left the shed door open and who in the world told you you could have that chicken wire?"

Then she knelt down and crawled through the hole in the hedge, disappearing into her own backyard.

"Let's go back and put the cage in the pond," Owen said.

But just as the boys reached the edge of the yard, thunder rumbled. Rain began to fall in big, slow drops.

Plunk.

Plunk.

Plunk.

And then the sky turned dark, lightning flashed, and the rain poured down, drenching the boys and sending them scurrying for shelter.

That night at supper, Owen told his parents about the frog cage while Earlene fumed by the stove.

His father thought it was a great idea.

His mother worried that the boys would fall in the pond.

Earlene mumbled about the chicken wire belonging to his grandfather and that mangy stray cat getting in the shed when Owen left the door open.

After supper, Owen took Tooley up to his bedroom and set him in the middle of the bed.

Tooley did a little half jump, then settled down in the folds of the quilted bedspread.

Owen inspected Tooley's froggy skin.

He rubbed his finger along Tooley's yellow throat.

He examined Tooley's big webbed feet.

He lifted Tooley and peered into his eyes.

Then he put the bullfrog into the tub in the closet and sat on the bed and worried.

Maybe Viola was right.

Maybe he should have used water from the pond in the tub instead of water from the hose.

Owen sat still and listened. The rain pattered against the window. Thunder rumbled in the distance. But inside the bedroom, it was quiet.

Owen sighed.

When he had first brought Tooley home, the frog had croaked all night long. That deep *r-u-u-u-m-m-m* sound that bullfrogs make.

But now he was quiet.

A flash of lightning lit up Owen's room. The rain beat harder against the window.

Tomorrow, Owen thought . . .

Tomorrow he had to do two things:

1. Get the frog cage into the pond so Tooley could move in and be happy.
2. Find the thing that had fallen off the train.

EIGHT

Y'all get out of my yard!" Joleen Berkus hollered through the screen door.

Owen cupped his hand over a grasshopper in the weeds and glared at her. Anybody who would tear down a perfectly good fort was deserving of a glare. Owen wondered what she had done with that trapdoor he had sawed into the wooden floor of his old bedroom or the ladder he and Travis and Stumpy had nailed to the back of the garage so they could climb up onto the roof.

"I said get out of my yard!" Joleen stormed out onto the porch and flapped a dish towel at the boys.

Travis yanked a small green cantaloupe off a tangled vine beside the birdbath and tossed it toward the porch. It landed on the walkway with a *thwump*.

Before Joleen could stomp down the steps, the boys

were clear across the street and around back of Stumpy's house, laughing so hard they could barely catch their breath. Then they jumped on their bikes and raced over to Owen's house.

As Owen pedaled, clutching a jar of grasshoppers in one hand, his stomach flipped and flopped with excitement. Today was the day they were going to put the cage in the pond.

They had made all kinds of plans for Tooley's new house. It would be attached to the side of the dock, one end in the shallow water and one end in the deeper water. There would be a log to sit on and rocks to hunker down beside and leaves to sleep on.

Water bugs and crickets and flies could go right through the chicken wire so Tooley would always have something tasty to snack on.

And every once in a while, the boys could open the top of the cage and take Tooley out and play with him.

It would be great.

"Let's go on down to the dock and start cutting the baling wire," Owen said after dropping two grasshoppers into the tub for Tooley.

He retrieved the baling wire and wire cutters from the shed, put them in a plastic grocery bag, and carefully closed the door behind him so Earlene wouldn't have anything to yammer about. Then he started across the yard with Travis and Stumpy behind him. But just as they got to the edge of the woods, Viola crawled through the hedge and said, "You should catch crawfish."

Owen sighed and rolled his eyes at Travis and Stumpy.

"Be quiet," Travis said.

"Yeah, be quiet," Stumpy said.

Viola eyed the grocery bag in Owen's hand.

"What's that?" she said.

"Nothing." Owen jiggled the bag at Viola. "Your mother's calling you," he said.

"Bullfrogs love crawfish," Viola said, pushing at her glasses. "I read it in the encyclopedia at my cousin's house."

Crawfish?

Really?

There were tons of crawfish in the creek beside Travis's house. Owen had caught about a million of them last summer. The boys had even had crawfish races and made trophies for the winners.

"You think you know everything, but you don't," Travis said.

"I know that bullfrogs don't want names and they don't want to live in cages and they love to eat crawfish." Viola lunged for the grocery bag in Owen's hand, but he yanked it away before she could grab it.

"Go away, *Vi-o-la*!" Owen hollered. Then he motioned for Travis and Stumpy to follow him and started down the path through the woods. After a few feet, he whirled around to see if Viola was following them.

She wasn't.

She was standing at the edge of the woods with that smug look on her smug face and sending irritation zipping down the path full steam ahead.

"She's gonna follow us," Stumpy said.

"Naw," Owen said as he stomped down the path, swinging the grocery bag. "When she goes in the woods, she gets wheezy and itchy. Besides, she hates the pond. There's too many gnats and too much mud and poison oak and all."

Owen hoped he was right.

But with a girl like Viola, you never knew.

"There!" Owen stood up and grinned down at the cage.

The perfect cage.

The cage where Tooley would live and be happy.

"Let's go get him!" he said, and raced up the path, through the woods, into the yard, and over to the back steps to the tub where Tooley sat, blinking up at the summer sky.

Pete and Leroy leaped off the porch, tails wagging, and trotted over to join the fun.

Owen lifted Tooley out of the tub.

The back door opened and Earlene stepped out of the house and glared down at him. Her eyes darted from him to Tooley to Travis to Stumpy and then to him again.

"You're not going back yonder to those train tracks, are you?" she said.

"No, ma'am."

She glared some more.

"You're not going out on that rotten ole dock, are you?"

"We're taking Tooley down to the pond." Owen held Tooley up so his froggy legs dangled.

Owen was a master of evasion.

He could evade a question better than anybody he knew.

But Earlene was persistent.

"You're not going out on that rotten ole dock, are you?" she asked again.

Owen's mind raced. He was thinking that maybe he needed to sharpen his evasion skills.

"We put the cage in the pond for Tooley," he said.

"You listen to me, Owen Jester," Earlene said. "I'm in no mood to be fishing three drowned boys out of that snake-infested pond."

Owen heard Travis and Stumpy shuffling in the dirt behind him.

Travis and Stumpy were scared of Earlene. They always left all of the evading to Owen.

"Yes, ma'am," Owen said, because what else could he say?

Earlene made a *hmmpf* noise and pressed her lips together in a thin, hard line.

Owen waited.

Earlene went back in the house, letting the screen door slam shut behind her.

Owen and Travis and Stumpy and Pete and Leroy raced to the pond with Tooley.

NINE

Owen lay on his stomach on the dock and peered into the murky water. Tooley sat on the bottom of the pond inside the perfect cage.

Owen nudged him gently with a stick. Tooley swam to the other side of the cage and nestled back down into the squishy mud.

"He likes it!" Owen grinned up at Travis and Stumpy.

But inside Owen, something was niggling at him.

A teeny tiny niggle.

Barely noticeable.

But a niggle, nonetheless.

The niggle was caused by a thought.

The thought was this: Maybe, just *maybe*, Tooley should not be in that perfect cage.

Maybe he should be swimming freely around Graham Pond. Gliding gracefully through the water. Floating among the rotting oak leaves that had settled on the surface. Sunning lazily on the moss-covered logs along the edges.

Instead of in a cage. (Even if the cage was perfect.)

Owen pushed the niggle away.

Then he tossed the stick into the pond and said, "Now we can go look for the thing that fell off the train."

Travis and Stumpy let out a whoop.

The three boys raced around the pond toward the train tracks.

"What's that?" Travis said, pointing to a clump of weeds beside the tracks.

Something shiny and round was nestled in among the prickery vines.

Owen ran over and examined it. "A hubcap. Shoot!" he said, kicking at the weeds.

The boys walked glumly along the side of the tracks. Every now and then, one of them spotted something and would point and holler and they'd all race over to examine it. But it was never anything that seemed like it might have fallen off the train and made the noise that Owen had heard.

The thud.

The crack of wood.

The tumble, tumble, tumble sound.

"Let's go to my house and get lunch," Stumpy said.

So the boys headed back up the path through the woods. But they hadn't gotten far when Owen stopped.

He snapped his fingers.

"Wait a minute!" he said.

Travis and Stumpy waited.

"Tumble, tumble, tumble," Owen said.

Travis and Stumpy waited some more.

"If something's tumbling, that means it's, like, rolling," Owen said.

Travis and Stumpy waited some more.

"So that means that whatever was tumbling was probably going downhill, right?"

Travis and Stumpy looked at each other.

"Yeah," they both said.

"So?" Travis said.

"So maybe whatever fell off the train isn't up by the tracks where we've been looking, but more downhill from the tracks, like in the bushes and stuff," Owen said.

Travis and Stumpy nodded and grinned and high-fived Owen and they all raced back to the tracks to search the bottom of the rocky, red-dirt slopes that ran along the sides.

They found a bicycle wheel with broken spokes.

They found a bullet-riddled stop sign.

They found the bent-up frame of an aluminum lawn chair.

They found a mildewed, mud-covered sofa cushion.

They found a grocery cart with two missing wheels.

They found cinder blocks and broken bottles and rusty cans.

"I'm sick of this," Travis said.

"Yeah," Stumpy said. "Me, too."

Owen's disappointment swirled around inside him and then settled with a heavy thunk in the pit of his stomach.

"Not me," he lied.

"I'm going home," Travis said.

"Me, too," Stumpy said.

"Not me." Owen jammed his hands into his pockets and strolled off, studying the ground, peering into the weeds and bushes, kicking at clods of dirt, pretending like he didn't care that Travis and Stumpy were quitters.

He glanced over his shoulder to see the two boys trotting up the tracks toward the path in the woods.

"Quitters," he muttered under his breath.

Owen climbed back up the slope and scanned the bottom of the ravine on the other side of the tracks.

It wasn't nearly as much fun searching without Travis and Stumpy.

But Owen was not a quitter.

While he searched, he thought about Tooley, and the niggle he had had earlier that day came back. The more he thought, the bigger the niggle got. It grew and grew until it became a tangled-up mass of worry. And in the center of the tangled-up mass was the biggest worry of all:

Maybe Tooley really *was* sad.

And then, just as Owen's stomach was beginning to ache, something caught his attention.

Something big.

Something red.

Down among the tangled bushes and scrub pines at the bottom of the ravine beside the tracks.

Owen hurried down the slope, slipping and sliding on the loose dirt and rocks, pushing through clumps of brush and weeds.

And then he stopped.

He stood in gape-mouthed wonder.

"Whoa!" he said out loud.

The tangle of niggling worry in his stomach disappeared.

Poof!

Because lying there before him was the thing that had fallen off the train.

Owen was sure of it.

CHAPTER
TEN

Owen scrambled through the thick brush, ducking under low-hanging branches and climbing over rotting logs. Prickers scratched his legs and snagged his clothes as he made his way toward the thing.

The thing that had fallen off the train.

The thing that had made the *thud*.

It was big and red and made of metal.

But what was it?

Next to it, jammed between two scraggly oak trees, was part of an enormous wooden crate. Scattered here and there among the brush and weeds surrounding it were pieces of wood, splintered and broken.

The crack of wood.

The red thing lay nestled at the bottom of the ravine,

where it had rolled down the slope from the railroad tracks.

The tumble, tumble, tumble sound.

One last push through the weeds and Owen was standing next to it.

His mind raced.

What *was* this thing?

One end was rounded, like the nose of an airplane.

On the other end was a small propeller.

On each side was a short, stubby wing.

There was a small propeller on each stubby wing.

Was this an airplane?

Owen didn't think so.

The wings weren't big enough.

There were no wheels, just a flat, box-shaped bottom.

Besides, it was surely too small to be an airplane. Owen could stand on tiptoe and see right over the top of it.

Then what was it?

Owen walked around it, studying it carefully. There was an enclosed compartment with three large windows in the front and one round, bubble-shaped window on each side.

In back of the enclosed compartment was a hollowed-out space. Strapped inside the space were four large tanks, like the kind that scuba divers use.

Painted on one side of the red thing, just under the bubble-shaped window, was a dolphin. A silvery dolphin swimming through blue ocean waves.

Above the dolphin, in swirling black letters, was written:

Water Wonder 4000

"A submarine!" Owen whispered.

This red thing that had fallen off the train was a submarine!

Owen peered through the windows. Inside was an instrument panel with a few glass-covered dials, some switches, and a joystick. In front of the instrument panel were two small seats.

A submarine just big enough for two people!

Owen had never seen anything like it.

He ran his hand along the side of the submarine, feeling the smooth metal, tracing the dolphin, brushing dirt off the rounded nose up front, turning the little propeller in back. He examined the top. There were a few small dents here and there. Some scratches in the shiny red paint. But other than that, the Water Wonder 4000 looked perfect.

Owen's heart was racing.

Wait . . .

. . . just *wait . . .*

. . . until Travis and Stumpy saw *this*!

Owen dashed across the yard toward the woods, followed by Travis and Stumpy. Pete and Leroy galloped along beside them, barking happily.

"Where are y'all going?"

Viola's voice sliced through the air.

Owen stopped.

Travis and Stumpy stopped.

Pete and Leroy ran in circles around them.

Owen's face twitched.

His fingers fluttered.

His feet bounced.

Why, why, why did Viola always have to show up at the wrong time?

He could hardly wait to show Travis and Stumpy the little red submarine.

He had told them he'd found the thing that had

fallen off the train, but he hadn't told them what it was.

He wanted to surprise them.

But now Viola was here, ruining everything like she always did.

"We're going to the pond to catch some snakes," Owen said. "Wanna come?"

Viola marched toward them, clomping across the yard in flowered rubber rain boots. "You are not," she said.

"We are, too," Travis said. "And then we're gonna dig up some big, fat worms for Tooley. Those slimy gray ones that live in the mud down there by the pond."

Viola narrowed her eyes and set her mouth in a thin, hard line. "Fibber," she said.

Owen couldn't keep still. He bounced from foot to foot.

"Come on with us, Viola," he said. "You can stick your arm down in the water and touch Tooley. If you're lucky, you won't get any leeches stuck on you."

"There's no leeches in that pond," Viola said.

Owen made a little *pfft* sound and rolled his eyes. "You think you know everything, but you don't," he said.

He nodded toward Travis. "Tell Viola about the leeches," he said.

Travis stared at Owen.

Owen winked a teeny tiny little wink and said, "You know, the *leeches*?"

"Oh!" Travis said. "You mean them nasty, slimy, squishy, juicy leeches that stick on you and suck all your blood out?"

Owen nodded solemnly. "Yep. That's the ones."

"There's leeches down there, all right," Travis said. "Gerald Asher's brother went fishing down there once and got a leech this big stuck on him." Travis held his hands out about a foot apart, then widened them a tad, then widened them a tad more until that leech was about a yard long.

Stumpy snorted with laughter and Owen shot him a look.

"Y'all must think I'm stupid," Viola said, resting one hand on her hip and cocking her head. Her voice had that usual know-it-all sound to it, but Owen was delighted to see that she had turned a little pale.

"We might even feed some leeches to Tooley," he said.

"Bullfrogs don't eat leeches," Viola said. "Besides, that frog does *not* want to be named Tooley. Trust me." She brushed a strand of hair out of her face and added, "*And* he should *not* be living in a cage."

Owen couldn't stand it another minute. The only thing left to do was to holler "Rocket!"

CHAPTER
ELEVEN

Just when Owen thought he could finally show Travis and Stumpy the submarine, Earlene's voice came thundering through the trees.

"Owen Jester!"

"Dang." Owen peeked out from under the branches of the oak tree tepee.

"Owen Jester!"

"Dang," Owen said again. Just when they had finally ditched Viola, here was Earlene messing things up.

"Owen Jester!" Earlene's voice was harsh and sharp.

"Coming!" Owen hollered.

Thunk.

Thunk.

Owen kicked the leg of his chair.

Swirl.

Swirl.

He circled his fork around on his plate, leaving a trail in the cold gravy.

"But why can't I just go check on Tooley?" he said.

His father shot him a stern glare.

His mother let out a heaving sigh.

Earlene harrumphed by the stove.

Owen hated Wednesday nights.

On Wednesday nights, the Jesters went to Fork Creek Baptist Church for Bible study.

Owen didn't care for Bible study.

He could never remember the Bible passages that he was supposed to recite.

He felt stupid acting out the parts in the Bible story skits.

He hated standing in a circle around the piano singing hymns.

Thunk.

Thunk.

Owen kicked the leg of his chair again.

This little light of mine,
I'm gonna let it shine.

Owen glanced around him.

All the other children were singing.

Miss Nora Haskins was playing the piano.

A couple of the goody-goody girls were clapping their hands and swaying from side to side.

Owen tugged at the stiff collar of his shirt and moved his mouth, pretend-singing.

He was good at pretend-singing.

Let it shine,

Let it shine,

Let it shine.

Owen's mind wandered.

Actually, it wasn't so much wandering as it was darting.

Back and forth.

Sometimes his mind darted to Tooley. Owen pictured the bullfrog sitting on the log inside the cage in the pond.

All alone.

Sad?

There was that niggle again.

Other times, his mind darted to the submarine.

The Water Wonder 4000.

Nestled there in the bushes below the train tracks.

Then the niggle about Tooley turned into a whir of excitement about the submarine.

Owen could hardly wait to show it to Travis and Stumpy.

But here he was, standing in a circle, pretend-singing.

"Amen!" Miss Nora Haskins sang out with one last, grand flourish of her fingers on the piano keys.

"Amen!" all the other children echoed.

"Amen," Owen muttered under his breath.

"Tell Grampa about the frog," Owen's mother said.

"Um, well . . ." Owen glanced at his grandfather's brown-spotted hand, resting on top of the pale blue blanket. Every now and then, his gnarly fingers twitched.

"I finally caught that big ole bullfrog down at Graham Pond." Owen's grandfather hadn't felt well enough to have visitors for a while, so Owen hadn't been able to tell him about Tooley.

He watched his grandfather's face.

Was he sleeping?

His grandfather took a wheezy breath in.

He let a wheezy breath out.

"And me and Travis and Stumpy made a cage for him out of that chicken wire in the barn," Owen said.

The stale air in the bedroom smelled like medicine and furniture polish.

Owen's mother fiddled with the blanket and fluffed the pillow.

Owen's grandfather's mouth turned up a teeny bit at the corners.

A smile?

"His name is Tooley Graham," Owen said.

His grandfather drew in a sharp breath and let out a gravelly "Huh!"

Then he opened his eyes and looked at Owen and nodded a little bit.

"Viola says he's sad, but you know how dumb she is."

"Owen!" His mother frowned over at him.

"Well, she is."

Owen's grandfather said "Huh!" again.

So Owen spent the rest of the evening sitting beside his grandfather's bed, telling him about Tooley.

He told him how there were a lot of bullfrogs in Graham Pond but that Tooley was the biggest and greenest and had a heart-shaped red spot between his eyes. He told him about how long it had taken to catch him and how he had made the two frog houses (the inside one and the outside one) and then the perfect chicken-wire cage down in the pond. He told him about how he and Travis and Stumpy caught crickets and flies and mosquitoes for him, but how Tooley didn't seem to have much of an appetite.

Owen's grandfather seemed to enjoy the conversation.

He even chuckled one time.

Owen told his grandfather everything he could think of to tell him . . .

. . . except . . .

. . . he did not tell him about the Water Wonder 4000.

That submarine was the biggest, most fantastic secret Owen had ever had in his whole life and he wasn't sharing it with anyone except Travis and Stumpy.

Owen was relieved when he finally saw the moon glowing in the darkening sky outside the bedroom window, signaling the end of the day.

First thing tomorrow, Owen was taking Travis and Stumpy down to the tracks to see the submarine.

CHAPTER
TWELVE

Whoa!" Travis said, thwacking his forehead with the palm of his hand.

"Whoa!" Stumpy said, arching his eyebrows in surprise.

Owen crossed his arms and grinned. "Know what it is?" he said.

Travis studied the little red submarine, peering in the windows, examining the scuba tanks.

Stumpy walked around it, patting the smooth metal sides, pushing on the propeller in the back.

"It's a submarine!" Owen said.

Travis shook his head in wonder.

Stumpy's jaw dropped.

The three boys chattered excitedly as they examined the Water Wonder 4000.

The rounded nose in front.

The stubby wings with the propellers on the sides.

The windowed compartment on top.

The little propeller in the back.

The scuba tanks.

Owen climbed up onto one of the stubby little wings and then crawled onto the top of the submarine, grinning down at Travis and Stumpy.

He was sure he had never, not ever, not even once, seen anything as perfectly, fantastically cool.

He jumped down off of the submarine, landing in the leaves with an *oomph*.

"Hey, wait a minute!" he said. "Where's the hatch?"

"The hatch?" Travis said.

"Yeah, you know, the *hatch*." Owen stood on tiptoe and ran his hand along the top. "How do you get in this thing?"

The boys looked and felt and studied, and then Owen dropped to his hands and knees and examined the bottom of the submarine.

"There!" he said. "You crawl up in there!" He pointed to an opening in the bottom.

The three boys knelt in the dirt and weeds and peered into the opening.

CHAPTER
THIRTEEN

O wen scrambled out of the submarine.

The boys poked each other and gestured and scurried behind a tangle of bushes.

"Owen, Travis, and Stumpy!" Viola called.

Owen put his finger to his lips and peeked out from behind the bushes. Viola was up on the train tracks above them.

He ducked back behind the bushes, his heart pounding and his stomach knotted with dread. He sent a silent message up through the trees to Viola:

Please, please, please . . .

Please don't see the submarine.

He peeked out again. Viola took a few steps.

Owen waited.

Was she leaving?

Viola stopped.

Owen waited.

"Your frog is sick, Owen," Viola called out, pushing at her glasses.

Owen's dread-filled stomach did a somersault.

Tooley!

He had been so excited about showing Travis and Stumpy the Water Wonder 4000 that morning that he hadn't even thought about checking on Tooley.

Niggle.

Niggle.

Owen looked at Travis and Stumpy. They stared back, wide-eyed, waiting.

Owen put his finger to his lips again.

And then he heard the sweet sound of Viola's sandals on the gravelly ground beside the tracks . . .

. . . walking away.

Phew!

When Owen was fairly certain that she was gone, he motioned for Travis and Stumpy to follow him. Then he scrambled up the side of the slope to the edge of the tracks. Viola was way off in the distance, running toward home.

"She's been to the pond!" Travis said with an

indignant stamp of his foot. "I thought you said she wouldn't never go down to the pond."

Owen let out a sigh and shook his head. "I didn't think she would."

"And you said she wouldn't never come back here to the railroad tracks," Travis said.

Owen shrugged. What could he say?

"What if she goes back to the pond and lets Tooley out of the cage?" Stumpy said.

"Naw, she wouldn't do that," Owen said. But his voice didn't sound nearly as convincing as he wanted it to.

Owen could only hope that the one good thing about Viola—her allergies—would kick in big-time and keep her away.

"Okay, listen," he said. "Here's what we gotta do. We gotta cover the submarine with branches and leaves and stuff so nobody will see it."

Travis and Stumpy nodded.

"Then," Owen said, "we gotta go check on Tooley."

Owen stroked Tooley's back. The bullfrog blinked.

One slow blink.

"Aw, he ain't sick," Travis said.

"Viola's dumb," Stumpy said.

Owen held Tooley up and examined his stomach, his throat, his legs.

The bullfrog wasn't quite as green as he used to be.

His throat wasn't quite as yellow as it used to be.

The heart-shaped spot between his eyes wasn't quite as red as it used to be.

Niggle.

Niggle.

"Maybe we should catch another frog to keep him company," Travis said.

"Maybe he needs a bigger cage," Stumpy said.

Owen put Tooley back in the cage and shut the lid. The frog climbed up on the log and stared out at the pond with dull yellow eyes.

"Let's go scoop up some water bugs over yonder on the other side of the pond," Owen said.

That night, Owen sat by his bedroom window.

The soft, steady chirp of crickets drifted up from the garden below.

Way off in the distance, a dog barked.

And then Owen heard a sound that made him sit up straighter and cock his head.

The deep *r-u-u-u-m-m-m* of a bullfrog.

Owen's heart did a little flip.

Was that Tooley?

Tooley making a bullfrog sound?

R-u-u-u-m-m-m.

There it was again.

And then . . .

. . . another frog joined in at the same time . . .

. . . and then another . . .

. . . until there seemed to be a whole chorus of bull-frogs.

Owen's niggle turned into a punch.

Ooomph!

Because Owen realized that all the other bullfrogs down there in the pond were free. Pushing their froggy legs through the dark water under the starry sky.

Calling out their froggy songs from a moonlit log.

But not Tooley.

Tooley was sitting glumly in his perfect cage.

FOURTEEN

After dumping a jar full of bugs through the chicken wire of Tooley's cage, Owen raced over to Tupelo Road to Stumpy's house.

A sprinkler *chug, chug, chugged* in circles in the yard while Owen, Travis, and Stumpy sat on the porch steps and talked about the submarine.

"Should we tell somebody about it?" Stumpy said.

Owen and Travis stared at Stumpy in disbelief.

Travis smacked him on the arm. "Heck, no!" he said.

"Not yet, anyways," Owen said.

Every now and then, Joleen Berkus appeared at her front door and glared over at the boys.

"I say we get that thing into the pond and go for a ride," Owen said.

"Heck, yeah!" Travis slapped his knee.

Stumpy frowned. "I don't know."

"Then stay home, diaper-head baby," Travis said. "Me and Owen'll do it, right, Owen?"

Owen's mind raced.

Could they really get the submarine into the pond?

How in the world would they get it there?

And even if they got it there, could they actually figure out how to make it run?

Could they *really* zip along under the water, gazing out at the pond from the bubble-shaped windows?

Owen nodded slowly. "Yeah," he said. "We *will* do it."

He and Travis slapped each other a high five and looked at Stumpy.

"You in or you out?" Owen said, holding his palm up.

Stumpy hesitated.

Then he slowly lifted his hand and lightly tapped Owen's palm with his own. "I'm in."

The boys huddled together up in the hayloft of the barn the rest of the morning, planning how they would get the Water Wonder 4000 down to the pond.

The good news was that the submarine was on the same side of the train tracks as the pond.

The bad news was that the submarine was probably heavy.

Real heavy.

The other bad news was that there were a lot of bushes and small scrub pines between the submarine and the pond.

The boys made lists of possible ways they could get the submarine down to the pond, like

Put the submarine on a wagon.

and

Pull the submarine behind a riding lawn mower.

Then they made lists of supplies they might need, like rope and chains and bungee cords.

Sometimes the idea of getting the submarine into the pond seemed like the greatest idea Owen had ever had.

Other times, it seemed stupid and impossible.

Then there was the problem of actually driving the submarine. Could they really figure out how to do it?

As if he had read Owen's mind, Travis said, "Do you think we can figure out how to make that sub run?"

Owen shrugged. "There's not that many switches

inside. Maybe we can just fiddle around with them a little bit."

"Maybe there's instructions somewhere," Stumpy said.

Owen and Travis stared at Stumpy.

Stumpy never had good ideas.

Stumpy never thought of stuff before Travis and Owen did.

But now he had.

"Instructions!" Owen said. "Yeah! I bet there's instructions somewhere!"

Owen and Travis high-fived Stumpy, and they all hurried out of the hayloft, whistled for Pete and Leroy, and raced across the yard, through the woods, and around the pond to the train tracks.

They scrambled down the slope toward the submarine.

And then . . .

. . . they stopped.

There in front of them, standing next to the Water Wonder 4000, staring through thick glasses with red-rimmed eyes, was Viola.

CHAPTER
FIFTEEN

Travis let a string of cusswords fly, and Stumpy broke off a branch and hurled it at Viola's feet while Owen stood stiff with anger, meeting Viola's fly-eyed gaze with narrowed eyes.

"I know what that is," she said, wiping her nose with the palm of her hand and nodding toward the Water Wonder 4000.

"Go away!" Owen yelled.

"That's a submarine," Viola said, and then whipped a tissue out of her pocket and blew her nose.

"Mind your own business," Travis snapped.

"Yeah!" Stumpy hollered.

"A submersible," Viola said.

The boys looked at each other.

"Go away," Owen said again, knowing full well that Viola wasn't going anywhere.

"It came from Canada." Viola waved a jagged-edged piece of wood at them. "This is the shipping label that was on the crate."

Travis narrowed his eyes. "What crate?"

"The crate the submarine was in, dummy," Viola said.

"Let me see that." Owen yanked the piece of wood out of Viola's hand and studied it.

Sure enough, a label with two addresses was on the wood.

The submarine had come *from* Water Wonder Technologies, Inc., in British Columbia, Canada.

It had been going *to* Sun and Sand Tropical Resort in Miami, Florida.

Owen hated it when Viola figured things out before he did.

"So what?" he said.

"So, you've got to tell somebody about this submarine." Viola wiped at her watery eyes.

"No way!" Travis said.

"Then that's the same as stealing." Viola gestured

toward the little red submarine. "I bet that cost a lot of money. You can't just keep it."

"We can do anything we want to. Right, Owen?" Stumpy said.

Owen tossed the piece of wood into the bushes. Pete and Leroy trotted over and sniffed it.

"Who said we're keeping it?" Owen said.

Travis and Stumpy looked at each other, then stared at Owen, waiting.

"Then what are you going to do about it?" Viola said.

"We're, um, we're going to, um . . ." Owen shuffled the toe of his sneaker in the leaves, his mind racing. "We're going to call the railroad company and tell them all about it," he said. "So you can go on home now."

He smiled at Viola.

A big, fake smile.

"Yeah," Travis said. "You can go on home now." He pushed Viola. Not hard. But just enough to make her stumble a little and send her glasses sliding down her nose.

"I know all about submarines," she said. "I did my science fair project on submarines last year. I know *everything* about them."

"You do not," Owen said.

But he knew she was right.

Viola was always right.

Owen was certain that Viola *did* know everything about submarines.

Viola knew everything about everything.

Aggravation swirled around inside Owen like a tornado.

Viola folded her arms and lifted her chin. "That's an ambient-pressure submarine," she said.

"There ain't no such thing as that!" Travis said.

Owen kicked a piece of gravel in her direction. "Go away," he said.

Viola sneezed. "Okay," she said. "I'll go tell Earlene y'all need the phone number of the railroad company so you can call them and tell them about the submarine." She pushed past the boys and started up the slope toward the tracks.

"Wait!" Owen called after her.

Viola turned. Little red splotches had begun to appear on her neck.

"Look, Viola," Owen said. "We *are* going to call the railroad company. We just want to check this thing out first." He lifted his eyebrows and waited.

Viola scratched her neck.

"So, just don't say anything to anybody about it, okay?" he said.

"Well . . ." Viola looked over Owen's shoulder at the submarine. "Maybe."

"What's wrong with your neck?" Stumpy said.

Viola scratched. "I'm allergic to pine," she said. "And ragweed and pigweed and—"

"Then you better go home before you die," Travis said.

Stumpy snorted.

Owen grinned.

Viola tossed her hair over her shoulder and stomped off toward home. But she hadn't gotten far when she whirled around and said, "Something's wrong with that frog of yours, Owen." She blew her nose, wiped her eyes, and added, "I know everything about frogs."

Owen's tornado of aggravation was spinning so fast it took all the words right out of his head. All he could think of to say was "You do not."

Which is exactly what he said.

"You do not!"

Owen watched Viola disappear up the tracks. Then he turned to Travis and Stumpy and said, "Let's get that submarine in the pond before Viola ruins everything."

CHAPTER
SIXTEEN

This is impossible," Travis said, wiping sweat off his forehead.

Stumpy plopped down in the pine needles and shook his head. "We can't do this," he said.

Owen examined the knot in the rope they had tied around the submarine. "Maybe we should bring the tractor down here," he said.

"There's too many trees and stuff in the way," Travis said. "Besides, you don't even know how to drive that tractor."

"I do so," Owen said. "Well, sort of." He had ridden on his grandfather's tractor a few times when his dad mowed the field behind the barn. He could probably figure out how to drive it. But Travis was right about the trees. It would be impossible to drive the tractor from the barn to the train tracks.

The boys had worked all afternoon.

First, they had searched inside the submarine for some kind of instructions about how to run it. They had looked under the seats and in the back between the scuba tanks and even in the bushes and weeds on the slope beside the tracks.

But they hadn't found a thing.

Owen had used his most convincing voice to assure Travis and Stumpy that they *would* figure out how to run the Water Wonder 4000, but they had to get it down to the pond first.

So they set to work tying rope around the submarine and trying to move it. They had actually managed to drag it a couple of feet, but it was obvious that the Water Wonder 4000 was just too heavy for them to get it all the way to the pond. And even if they could pull it, they were going to have to cut down some trees and bushes to clear a path first.

"Okay," Owen said, "here's what we've got to do." He snapped a couple of branches off a scraggly pine tree. "We've got to get some saws and clippers and stuff and start clearing a path."

"That'll take forever," Travis said.

"No, it won't." Owen pulled at a tangle of vines. "There's three of us. We just have to find some good tools."

"What about my dad's Weedwhacker?" Stumpy said.

Owen shook his head. "Naw. Earlene'll hear that. We just need saws and hedge clippers and stuff like that."

The boys bumped their fists together while agreeing to meet in the barn later that day. Then they raced home to see what tools they could find to clear a path.

Owen stashed some tools in the corner of the barn and then headed down to the pond to check on Tooley. He sat on the rotting dock and stared glumly out across the water. The air was thick with heat. A shiny black turtle was sunning on a log at the edge of the pond. A bullfrog floated among a cluster of leaves nearby. Owen could just make out its bulging yellow eyes and the top of its green head.

Maybe he should try to catch that frog so Tooley would have a friend.

Owen sighed.

His niggle came back.

The niggle had started as a tiny seed of a thought.

Then it had begun to grow, bigger and bigger, until it became a full-grown thought.

Maybe he should let Tooley go.

Owen looked down into the cage. Tooley floated in the dirty water, nestled up against the side, one webbed foot resting on the chicken wire.

He looked terrible.

Owen felt terrible.

He had worked so hard to catch that frog. He had stalked him for weeks, scanning the edges of the pond, searching the leaves and logs. It had been so much fun, trying to figure out if the frog he spotted was *his* frog. The one with the heart-shaped red spot between his eyes.

And then, when he had finally caught him, he had figured Tooley Graham would be his forever.

But now Owen was starting to think maybe he had made a mistake.

He reached into the water and touched Tooley's foot. The frog swam lazily to the other side of the cage . . .

. . . away from Owen.

"Tooley Graham," Owen whispered.

The frog nestled down into the slimy mud on the bottom of the pond and closed his eyes.

Owen let out a sigh so big and so loud that the turtle scampered off the log and into the pond, sending little ripples across the surface of the water.

Owen whispered "Tooley Graham" one more time before trudging slowly back up the path to meet Travis and Stumpy in the barn.

CHAPTER
SEVENTEEN

Owen and Travis and Stumpy sawed and clipped and dug and hacked.

They sawed down scruffy little pine trees.

They clipped overhanging branches.

They dug up clumps of thorny bushes.

They hacked at tangled vines.

Pete and Leroy joined them from time to time, chewing on twigs, rooting their noses in the freshly dug dirt, then scampering back through the woods toward home again.

Inch by inch, the three boys were clearing a path from the submarine to the pond. By the time the afternoon sun had begun to sink, the backs of their necks were burned and they were only halfway there.

Travis tossed a saw onto a clump of vines. "That's it," he said. "I'm sick of doing this."

"Me, too," Stumpy said, leaning on the garden hoe he had been using to hack up the roots of a bush.

"We can't stop now," Owen said. "We're almost halfway there."

"It's too hot," Travis said. "We can work on it some more in the morning, when it's cooler." He picked up the saw and tossed it into the wheelbarrow with a clang. "Besides," he added, "we don't even know how we're going to get that sub down to the pond, anyways."

Stumpy nodded in agreement.

"And," Travis went on, "even if we do get it to the pond, we don't even know how to drive it." He tossed another tool into the wheelbarrow. "I'm going home."

"Me, too," Stumpy said.

Quitters, Owen thought.

But he wasn't about to say it out loud. If he did, they were liable to quit for good.

All he could do was let out a big, heavy sigh and help them load the tools into the wheelbarrow and head back to the barn.

But just as they had finished stashing the tools

under a tarp in the corner of the barn, Owen's mood went from bad to worse.

Viola stepped through the barn door and said, "So, what are y'all gonna do about that submarine?"

Owen pushed past her and stormed out, followed by Travis and Stumpy.

Viola hurried after them. "I know what y'all are doing," she said.

Owen whirled around. "You want a trophy, Viola?"

Much to Owen's surprise, Viola blushed. "What do you mean?" she said.

"I mean, a trophy for being Genius of the World or something," Owen snapped.

Travis and Stumpy slapped their knees, sputtering with laughter.

"You said you were going to call the railroad company and tell them about that submarine," Viola said.

"I *am*," Owen said, and marched off toward the back porch and sat on the bottom step. Travis and Stumpy did the same.

Viola stood in the middle of the yard with her hands on her hips while the three boys tried to ignore her.

"Y'all are clearing trees and stuff so you can get that submarine down to the pond," she called over to them.

Owen jumped up and hissed, "Shhhhh!"

He shot a quick look up at the back door, hoping like anything that Earlene wasn't standing there.

She wasn't.

Owen moved closer to Viola and whispered, "Look, Viola, somebody's gonna have to come get that submarine, right?" He glanced up at the back door again. "I mean, after I call the railroad company and tell them about it," he added.

Viola shot a look at Travis, then Stumpy, then back at Owen. "So, why are you clearing stuff out of the woods?"

"We're just trying to help."

"I'm not stupid, Owen," she said.

"No, you're just dumb," Stumpy called from the back steps. He and Travis pushed each other and roared with laughter.

"Don't worry," Owen said. "Me and Travis and Stumpy are taking care of everything, okay?"

Viola narrowed her eyes and cocked her head. "Just

admit it, Owen," she said. "Y'all are going to put that submarine in the pond, aren't you?"

Silence.

Viola whirled around and stomped off toward the hedge, calling over her shoulder, "I'm telling on y'all!"

"Wait!" Owen hollered.

Viola stopped.

Owen ran over to her, his mind racing. He had to think of some way to keep Viola from ruining everything with the submarine.

"Look, Viola," Owen said. "We *are* going to call the railroad company. I swear." He held his hand up and looked solemnly at Viola.

"But you're going to put it in the pond first, aren't you?" she said.

Owen glanced over at Travis and Stumpy, then he said, "Yes."

Travis stamped his foot. "Dang, Owen!" he said.

"I knew it!" Viola gave Owen one of her smug faces.

"Trust me, Viola," Owen said. "We're going to take care of everything." He wiggled his eyebrows at her. "Okay?"

The silence hung thick and heavy in the summer air. Owen studied Viola's freckled face, her glasses perched down on the end of her nose. He had an uneasy feeling about her. She was liable to tell somebody about the submarine before he had a chance to get it in the pond.

Owen made an instant decision to take a gamble. "You can help us if you want to," he said. "Get some tools and meet us down there tomorrow."

Travis and Stumpy stopped laughing and stared at Owen, wide-eyed and openmouthed. Owen shot them a look that said, *Trust me, I know what I'm doing.*

Viola flapped her hand at Owen. "Yeah, right," she said. "Like I want to spend my day cutting down trees. Besides," she added, "you don't even know if that submarine works. Y'all are stupid to do all that work cutting down trees and stuff before you even *test* it."

"Aw, heck," Owen said. "That's a piece of cake. We got all that stuff figured out."

"Well, good luck," Viola said, turning to leave.

Owen tried not to look too relieved.

"If you change your mind, just come on down," he called after her.

As soon as Viola disappeared through the opening into her yard, Travis and Stumpy hurried over to Owen.

"What the heck did you do *that* for?" Travis said.

"Do what?" Owen said.

"Tell her she could help us."

"Because . . ." Owen beamed at Travis and Stumpy. "If she thinks she's in on our plan, she'll keep her yap shut and won't tell on us." Owen said this with an air of confidence, but on the inside, he had some big worries about trusting Viola. "Besides," he added, "I know Viola better than anybody. There is no way she's going to go down there in those woods and help us."

CHAPTER
EIGHTEEN

I got Jarvis's hacksaw," Viola said when she stepped out of the woods into the clearing. "I decided to come help y'all, after all."

Owen's stomach sank clear down to his feet.

Travis and Stumpy stared at Viola with their mouths hanging open.

Then Travis's face turned red and he stomped over to Owen. "Way to go, Owen!" he hollered. "*Now* what are we gonna do?"

Owen looked down at his feet, his mind racing. His sneakers were coated with dirt, his legs scraped and bruised. He looked at his hands, red and blistered. Sawing and clipping and digging and hacking was hard work. Much harder than he had thought it would be.

He and Travis and Stumpy had gotten to the

clearing early that morning, when the dew was still clinging to the wildflowers and ferns. But they hadn't made much progress. The ground was hard and full of rocks and roots. Some of the bushes pulled right up, but others had to be dug and chopped and yanked. Even the smallest trees required sawing and hacking. Branches had to be hauled off to the side. Large rocks had to be rolled away.

"I got Jarvis's hacksaw," Viola repeated, waving it in the air. She was wearing garden gloves that were way too big and a khaki canvas hat pulled down over her ears.

"Great," Owen said glumly. He flung his arm in the direction of one of the larger pine trees. "Then cut that down."

"Okay." Viola ran over to the tree and started sawing.

"Closer to the bottom," Owen said. "You can't leave a big ole stump there."

Owen looked at Travis and shrugged. What else could he do? Besides, they *could* use Viola's help. Why not let her do all the hard work with the larger trees and bushes? Maybe inviting Viola to help really *had* been a good idea.

But Travis and Stumpy didn't look like they thought Viola helping was a good idea. They looked like they were mad as all get-out.

While Viola happily sawed away at the tree, Owen whispered to Travis and Stumpy, explaining to them why Viola helping them was a good idea.

". . . and *then*," he whispered, "we'll only have to work on these puny little bushes while she does all the hard stuff."

He grinned.

Stumpy looked convinced, but Travis was still red-faced, glaring over at Viola and looking like he was ready to storm out of there.

". . . and *then*," Owen whispered, "we'll tell her we changed our minds about putting the submarine in the pond and that the railroad company is sending someone to pick it up in a couple of days, so she doesn't need to come back down here. And *then*"—he glanced over at Viola, who had paused from her sawing to blow her nose—"we can figure out how to get the submarine into the pond and go for a ride!"

Owen watched Travis's face change ever so slowly from mad-as-all-get-out to maybe-that-will-work.

So the boys picked up their tools and set to work sawing and clipping and digging and hacking again.

That night after dinner, Owen sat by his grandfather's bed and told him some more about Tooley.

He told him about how Tooley wasn't quite as green as he used to be.

How his throat wasn't quite as yellow and the heart-shaped spot wasn't quite as red.

He told him about how Tooley didn't seem to be eating the water bugs and crickets in the cage and how he didn't swim very much anymore.

"And last night," Owen said, "I heard some other bullfrogs down there in the pond and, well, um, I felt kind of bad."

Owen's grandfather raised his bushy white eyebrows.

"I mean, you know . . ." Owen picked at the dirt under his fingernails. "'Cause those other frogs were free, but, um, Tooley's in a cage."

His grandfather's mouth was a little droopy on one side. He nodded at Owen.

Owen could hear his mother out in the hall putting

sheets and pillowcases in the linen closet. He leaned toward his grandfather's bed and said in a low voice, "I'm thinking maybe I should let him go."

There.

He had said it.

The thought that had been niggling at him for so long.

And now that he had said it, he felt better.

That night, the train clattered down the tracks behind the house.

The *clatter, clatter, clatter* started low and got louder and louder until it became a *whoosh* and then trailed off to a faint *clatter, clatter, clatter* again.

And then it was gone.

As Owen sat in the window of his bedroom, breathing in the scent of honeysuckle and new-mown grass, listening to the crickets and bullfrogs, he knew he had to do two things.

He had to let Tooley go . . .

. . . and . . .

. . . he had to get that submarine into the pond.

NINETEEN

Owen had begged and pleaded and begged and pleaded to stay home from church.

Begging and pleading almost never worked.

But today a miracle had happened.

His mother had said yes!

So he and Travis and Stumpy had worked all morning, sawing and clipping and digging and hacking.

Viola had come down there to tell them she had to go over to Macon with her cousin but they could use Jarvis's hacksaw if they wanted to.

Travis had told her they didn't need her and they definitely didn't need anything that belonged to her loser brother, Jarvis.

After a while, they had gotten tired of sawing and clipping and digging and hacking, so they gathered around the Water Wonder 4000 to figure out how they were going to get it down to the pond once they were finished clearing the trees and bushes.

"Maybe we could take the wheels off a wagon, tie 'em on the sides, and just roll it," Stumpy said.

"That's dumb," Travis said. He slapped the side of the submarine, making a hollow, clanging noise that echoed through the trees.

"Yeah," Owen said, "that *is* pretty dumb, Stumpy."

Stumpy shrugged.

"Maybe we could pull it behind our bikes," Owen said.

Travis rolled his eyes.

"What if we got some more kids to help us pull it?" Travis said.

Owen shook his head. "Naw, this is our secret," he said. "Other kids'll just mess things up."

"Like Viola?" Travis said.

Owen blushed. He *had* messed things up by letting Viola get involved, but Travis didn't have to keep reminding him.

Stumpy pushed on the submarine with his foot. "It's just too heavy," he said. "We'll never do it."

"Yes, we will," Owen said.

"And then you're just going to drive it all around the pond like you know all about driving a submarine, right, Owen?" Travis asked as he hurled a stick over the top of the Water Wonder 4000.

"Look," Owen snapped, "if y'all don't want to help me anymore, then go on home. *I'm* the one that found this submarine and *I'm* going to get it in the pond and *I'm* going to take it for a ride with or without y'all." He stomped through the weeds and scrambled up the slope toward the train tracks.

"Wait!" Travis called after him.

Owen stopped.

"Okay," Travis said, "we'll help. But we've got to figure out how to do it."

"We *will*," Owen said, stamping his foot.

Travis and Stumpy joined Owen up by the tracks. They stood in silence, looking down at the submarine, so red and shiny and fantastic. The silver dolphin sparkled in the sun that filtered through the trees.

"Let's go up to the hayloft and think of some more ideas," Owen said.

So they headed to the barn and climbed up the ladder to the hayloft. They took out the list of ideas they had made earlier and sat on the dusty wooden floor and studied them. They talked about them and added to them and argued about them until they were all just plain sick of it.

"I'm sick of this," Travis said.

"Me, too," Stumpy said.

Owen had to admit, he was sick of it, too. He didn't want to keep *talking* about getting the submarine into the pond.

He wanted to *get* the submarine into the pond.

"Let's go check on Tooley," he said.

So the boys climbed down out of the hayloft, tucked the wrinkled notebook paper with their list of ideas under the tarp with the tools, and headed to the pond.

Owen lifted Tooley out of the cage and set him on his lap. The bullfrog settled down in the folds of Owen's shorts and closed his eyes.

"Do you think he's sick?" Owen said.

"Naw." Travis nudged Tooley gently with his finger. "He's just tired."

"Let's make the cage bigger," Stumpy said.

"Yeah," Travis said. "We could make it go all the way around the dock."

But Owen kept quiet.

He knew that Tooley didn't need a bigger cage.

He knew that Tooley needed to be free.

He needed to swim around Graham Pond with the other frogs.

He needed to climb on the logs and float on the leaves and nestle in the mud and eat the bugs . . .

. . . but not in a cage.

"We could catch more frogs and have a whole frog town!" Stumpy said.

"Yeah!" Travis tossed a rock into the middle of the pond.

Ploink.

Tooley opened one eye . . .

. . . and then closed it.

Travis and Stumpy went on and on about the frog town they could make and how it could have little froggy apartments made out of logs and froggy restaurants where the bugs would be and there could even be a froggy mayor.

"Tooley!" Stumpy said. "Tooley could be the mayor."

But Owen kept quiet.

He knew that Tooley didn't want to be the mayor of Frog Town.

Tooley wanted to be free.

Eat your squash," Earlene snapped.

Owen looked down at the blob of yellow mush on the plate in front of him.

Earlene rattled pans and clanged spoons and mumbled to herself while she huffed around the kitchen.

She was annoyed that Owen had managed to beg and plead his way out of church that morning.

She was annoyed that he had stayed gone all day without telling anybody where he was.

And she was annoyed that he didn't want to eat that blob of nasty squash.

"We're leaving for church in five minutes," Owen's mother called from upstairs.

The Jesters always went to church twice on Sundays. Once in the morning and once in the evening. Owen was still amazed that his begging and pleading had worked that morning, but he knew there was no way he was going to get out of going to church that evening.

"Eat your squash," Earlene snapped again.

Owen dipped the tip of his fork into the yellow mush and then dabbed it onto his tongue.

That seemed to annoy Earlene even more. She yanked the plate off the table, muttering about starving children somewhere in the world, and dumped the squash into the dog bowl.

"Go get ready for church," she said.

While Mrs. Suttles put a smiley-face sticker on his Bible-passage work sheet, Owen stared out the window and thought about Tooley.

He had been thinking and thinking and thinking and, somewhere between listening to Travis and Stumpy talk about Frog Town and swirling his fork around in Earlene's mushy yellow squash, he had made a decision.

As soon as he got home from church, he was going to go down to the pond and let Tooley go.

So now he was sitting on a metal chair in the basement of Fork Creek Baptist Church, wishing Mrs. Suttles would hurry up with those smiley-face stickers and hoping, hoping, hoping that his parents didn't want to stay for Bible Bingo.

Sometimes they did.

If they stayed for Bible Bingo, it would be dark when they got home and he wouldn't be allowed to go down to the pond.

Owen stood in a circle with the other kids as they said some prayers and sang some songs and then they were finally done. He raced upstairs to find his parents, hoping, hoping, hoping they were not sitting at the Bible Bingo table.

They weren't.

Owen said a silent *yahoo* in his head and raced out to the car.

As the sun sank lower in the sky, the pond seemed to be settling in for the night.

The moss-covered logs along the edges were empty. No turtles basking in the summer sun.

The water was still and smooth as glass. No water bugs leaving ripples across the surface.

Not a single pair of yellow bullfrog eyes peering out from the floating leaves that gathered in clumps in the shadows.

The low hum of crickets was starting, interrupted from time to time by the buzz of a mosquito.

Owen lifted the lid of the perfect cage.

He reached in and scooped Tooley up. Then he sat on the end of the dock and had a little chat with the big green bullfrog.

He told him about how much fun it had been to come down to the pond every day and look for him.

He praised him for his ability to avoid being captured for so long. The way he had darted out of the net quick as lightning. The way he had shot out from under the colander.

And then he apologized for a few things.

"I'm sorry I made you stay in that cage so long," Owen said to Tooley. "Viola said you never wanted to be Tooley Graham and that you just want to be a frog," Owen said. "So, well, if that's true, and, um, I guess maybe it is 'cause Viola's almost always right even though she's so dumb, well, anyway, I'm sorry about that."

The frog moved a little in Owen's lap.

"And, um . . ." Owen stroked Tooley's back. "I'm sorry if I made you sad."

Owen leaned over the edge of the dock and lowered Tooley into the water.

"Goodbye, Tooley," he said.

Then he let go of the most beautiful bullfrog in Carter, Georgia, and watched as it pushed its long froggy legs and disappeared into the pond without so much as a splash.

TWENTY-ONE

Owen knew Travis and Stumpy would be mad as hornets that he had let Tooley go.

But he didn't care.

Tooley had been *his* frog, not theirs.

Travis stomped around the dock muttering "Dang it!" and "No fair!" and Stumpy glared and repeated everything Travis said.

"And then we spent half the dern summer building that cage!" Travis hollered.

"Yeah!" Stumpy hollered.

Owen looked at the perfect cage attached to the edge of the dock.

The *empty* perfect cage.

Then he gazed out across the pond, wishing he could

see into the murky water and catch a glimpse of Tooley, swimming happily with the other frogs, resting peacefully among the rotting leaves on the muddy bottom. Maybe enjoying a snack, chomping on a juicy cricket.

"You think your stupid girlfriend, Viola, is right about everything," Travis snapped.

"She's not my girlfriend," Owen said.

"She is, too," Stumpy said.

"She is not!"

Back and forth and on and on they went, arguing and hollering and snapping and accusing until they all just ran out of steam and fell silent.

A dragonfly hovered in the air in front of them, then flitted off to the other side of the pond.

"So, um, are y'all still going to help me with the submarine?" Owen said.

"Get your girlfriend to help you," Travis said. Then he stormed past Owen and headed up the path into the woods.

Stumpy stood there for a minute, looking down at his feet, then said, "Uh, see ya," before heading off up the path after Travis.

Owen looked for the biggest rock he could find and

hurled it with all his might into the pond. It hit with a loud *ploink*, sending a spray of water into the air.

Now what was he going to do?

How was he ever going to get that submarine into the pond?

Owen sawed and clipped and dug and hacked all by himself. He hummed as he worked. And with each branch he sawed and each thorny bush he dug up, he began to feel better . . .

. . . until Viola stepped out of the woods and said, "I'm here!"

Owen groaned.

"Y'all got a lot done yesterday," Viola said, glancing around her.

Owen tossed a tangle of branches onto a pile of brush at the edge of the clearing. "Look, Viola," he said. "If you want to help, then help, but don't talk."

"Why are you so mean?" Viola said, putting on her dirty work gloves.

Owen didn't answer.

In fact, Owen didn't answer any of the gazillion questions Viola asked.

He didn't answer when she asked where Travis and Stumpy were.

He didn't answer when she asked if he had called the railroad company yet.

And he didn't answer when she asked if he was going to the pond to visit that sad old frog of his later that day.

Owen wasn't going to say one word to Viola.

But then . . .

. . . she went and said something that made him change his plans.

"I know how to get that submarine down to the pond."

Owen stopped his sawing.

He studied Viola.

Her big fly-eyes peering at him through her thick glasses.

Her freckly white legs.

Her know-it-all face.

"How?" he said.

TWENTY-TWO

Owen sat on a patch of moss beside the Water Wonder 4000 and listened to Viola going on and on in her schoolteacher voice.

About the ancient Egyptians.

About pyramids.

About simple machines.

Blah.

Blah.

Blah.

"Are you even *listening* to me, Owen?" she said, jabbing a finger at him. Her eyes were red and watery. Every few minutes, she wiped at her nose with a balled-up tissue.

"Look, Viola," he said. "I don't even know what the

heck you're talking about. What do Egyptians have to do with anything?"

So Viola explained it again.

"Some people think that the Egyptians moved those big stones for their pyramids by rolling them on logs." She went to the front of the submarine and squatted down. "See, we get some logs and we put them under the front." She patted the ground. "*Then*, we pull the submarine over the logs, which will be easy because the logs will roll."

She stood up and brushed dirt off her knees. "Then, as it rolls along, we take logs from behind it and move them back up to the front again . . . until we get to the pond."

A lightbulb went on.

Owen got it.

He snapped his fingers. "*Roll* it to the pond! Yeah!" He jumped up and ran over to the submarine. "And the pond is downhill from here, so that'll make it even easier."

Owen couldn't control himself.

He beamed at Viola.

Viola beamed back.

Owen sure was glad Travis and Stumpy weren't here to see all this beaming.

"Now we just have to get some logs," Viola said, rubbing her watery eyes and scratching at the pink rash that had appeared on her neck.

Owen's beam disappeared in a snap.

"How are we supposed to do that?" he said.

"Well, um . . ." Viola looked up into the trees. "We could . . . um . . . well . . . let's see . . ."

Owen never would have believed this day would come . . .

. . . the day Viola didn't know everything.

It figured.

All those times she had irritated the heck out of him by knowing everything and now here was the one time he *needed* her to know everything and she didn't.

And then, a lightbulb went on again.

"Pipes!" he said.

Viola stared at him through her thick glasses. "Pipes?"

"Yeah, you know, pipes. Like water pipes." Owen jerked his head in the direction of the new subdivision out by the main highway. "They're putting in a water line over on Sycamore Road and there's tons of PVC pipes just laying there in the ditch."

"That's perfect!" Viola said.

They beamed at each other again.

"There's only one problem," Viola said.

Owen rolled his eyes. Here was Miss Know-It-All again.

"We can't do it by ourselves," she said.

"Why not?"

"Look, Owen," she said. "Even if we could get enough pipes down here, we'd need help pulling that thing." She flung her arm in the direction of the submarine. "We'd need two people pulling and two people moving the pipes from the back to the front."

Dang it!

Viola was right again.

"We need Travis and Stumpy," she said.

"No way," Owen said. "They're quitters."

"Then we'll have to find somebody else." Viola squeezed her lips together and came close to making that smug face that Owen hated.

He shook his head. "If we tell anybody else, some grownup is gonna find out, for sure, and then everything'll be messed up."

"Then we need Travis and Stumpy," Viola said.

Owen sighed.

Then, as if Viola hadn't irritated him enough, she said, "You *are* going to make sure that submarine works before you try to move it, right?"

"Well, um, yeah, um, sure," he said.

Viola lifted her eyebrows and looked at Owen with her fly-eyes.

"Then do it now," she said. "Go on in there and start that thing up."

Owen looked over at the Water Wonder 4000. He had crawled up inside it lots of times now. He had studied the switches, examined the gauges, fiddled with the joystick. But could he actually *start* that submarine? Could he really make it run? Maybe he was just going to have to float around inside the submarine in the pond and not actually drive it.

"I will," Owen said. "As soon as we get Travis and Stumpy back down here."

Owen wasn't in the mood for Earlene's grumpiness.

When she snapped at him about the dirt he had tracked into the house, he shrugged.

When she lectured him about the dangers of the rotting floorboards in the hayloft, he nodded.

And when she gave him the evil eye for spilling milk on the kitchen table, he just said, "Heh."

Then he wiped up the milk, swept up the dirt, motioned for Pete and Leroy, and went outside to sit on the back steps and hope that Viola stayed away.

But Owen only sat on the back steps for about a minute. His insides were just too wound up to sit still.

It had been more than a week since he had first heard the thud, the crack of wood, the tumble, tumble, tumble sound.

The sound of the submarine falling off the train.

Somebody was going to be looking for that submarine. Owen was sure of it.

If he was going to get the Water Wonder 4000 into Graham Pond, he was going to have to do it soon.

But there were so many problems.

How was he going to convince Travis and Stumpy to help him when they were so mad at him for letting Tooley go?

And even if they agreed to help, could the four of them actually get the submarine to the pond?

And if they *did* get the submarine to the pond, would he really be able to drive it?

Problems.

Problems.

Problems.

But Owen was determined.

If he didn't do this now, when would he ever have another chance to drive a little submarine around in a pond?

Never.

He would never have a chance to do something like that ever again.

Owen strolled around the yard, kicking at dirt and tossing sticks for Pete and Leroy to chase.

Then he headed down to the woods and made his way along the path toward the train tracks. Pete and Leroy darted in and out of the woods, eager to chase anything Owen happened to throw, pinecones, sticks, even rocks.

Then, just as Owen neared the fork in the path, Leroy came leaping out of the woods with something in his mouth.

Not a pinecone.

Not a stick.

Not a rock.

But something made of paper.

"What's that?" Owen said, clapping his hands for Leroy to come to him.

The dog trotted happily over and sat in front of Owen, his tail swishing back and forth in the pine needles on the path.

"Let me see that, fella," Owen said.

Leroy had brought Owen a warped and wrinkled paperback book.

Owen brushed dirt off the book and examined it.

On the cover was a picture.

A picture of the Water Wonder 4000.

Above the picture were two words that made Owen let out a whoop that echoed through the trees.

The two words were

OPERATOR'S MANUAL

CHAPTER
TWENTY-THREE

Owen lay on his stomach in the hayloft and read the operator's manual for the submarine . . .

. . . starting with "Chapter 1: Getting to Know Your Water Wonder 4000" . . .

. . . and ending with "Chapter 6: Safety Tips and Troubleshooting."

Owen didn't understand some of the stuff.

Actually, Owen didn't understand a *lot* of the stuff.

There were sections on ambient pressure and buoyancy and ballasts and lots of other things he had never heard of. But there was plenty of stuff that seemed easy enough and made Owen think he really could do this.

He *could* drive the submarine around Graham Pond.

He tucked the manual under his shirt, climbed down out of the hayloft, jumped on his bike, and raced over to Tupelo Road.

Travis and Stumpy were building a skateboard ramp in the middle of the road while Joleen Berkus hollered at them.

"I'm gonna call the police," she hollered from her front porch.

Stumpy looked a little nervous, but Travis just hammered away without even a glance in her direction.

Owen's bike skidded to a stop, sending gravel and dirt flying.

Travis stopped hammering.

"Hey," Owen said.

Travis just lifted his eyebrows.

"Guess what?" Owen grinned at them.

"What?" Stumpy said.

"Leroy found the operator's manual for the submarine." Owen took the wrinkled book out from under his shirt and held it up for them to see.

Stumpy tossed his hammer aside and said, "Cool!"

But Travis stayed quiet.

So Owen took a deep breath and went to work on Travis.

He told him how the submarine only needed three feet of water to float.

How those air tanks were already filled and ready to go.

How there were just three switches to flip on the control panel.

Owen sort of hurried over some of the stuff, like about flooding the ballasts and adjusting the buoyancy control, since he didn't really get that part yet, and then he slowed down so he could be real dramatic when he told the part about using the joystick to go up and down and forward and back.

"It's easy!" Owen said. *"And,"* he added, jabbing his thumbs at himself, "I figured out how to get the sub down to the pond."

Travis kept his mouth set tight and his eyes narrowed.

Owen waited.

Stumpy looked from Travis to Owen and back to Travis.

"So . . ." Owen said. "You in or you out?"

"I'm in," Stumpy said.

Then Owen and Stumpy looked at Travis and waited.

Joleen Berkus hollered something from her front porch, but the three boys just ignored her.

"What about Viola?" Travis said.

"Oh, yeah," Stumpy said. "What about Viola?"

"Look," Owen said. "We need her to help us. It's gonna take four people. Besides . . ." Owen looked down at the operator's manual in his hand. "She *does* know a lot about some of this stuff."

Then Owen tossed in a heartfelt "Come on, Travis," and waited.

A dog barked.

A fly buzzed.

Joleen Berkus slammed her front door.

And Travis said, "Okay."

That night, the train rumbled along the tracks behind the house, while Owen stared up at the ceiling of his bedroom.

His grandfather's rhythmic snores drifted through the dimly lit hallway outside his door.

And from way down at the pond came the low, steady *r-u-u-u-m-m-m* of a bullfrog.

Tooley.

Owen was sure of it.

Then he took a flashlight out of the drawer of his bedside table and studied the operator's manual for the Water Wonder 4000 late into the night.

CHAPTER
TWENTY-FOUR

Owen and Travis sat inside the Water Wonder 4000, while Viola and Stumpy stood beside it, peering in the window.

Viola read from the operator's manual. "Before launching your Water Wonder 4000," she read, "there are a few simple tests to perform."

"Just get to the directions," Owen called through the window.

"Turn on the two breakers," Viola said.

Owen found the switches labeled BREAKER and pushed them on.

Click.

"Now flip the switch marked CONTROL PANEL."

Owen flipped the switch, and the control panel lit

up, filling the little compartment inside the submarine with a soft orange glow.

Owen and Travis high-fived each other.

Stumpy danced around in a circle, chanting, "It works! It works! It works!"

"Now flip on the Auto Depth Control and the Electronic Buoyancy Control switches," Viola said.

Owen did each thing that Viola read from the operator's manual.

He pushed the joystick forward, making the little propeller on the back of the submarine spin.

He pushed the thumb switch on the joystick, making the little propellers on the wings spin.

The soft hum of the motor made Owen's stomach flip with excitement.

Next, he opened the valves in the air tanks, while Viola continued to read.

"Now you have to open the ballast blow valves," she said.

Travis turned the valves, and both boys jumped as a blast of air entered the tanks.

"Turn on the flow meter so air for breathing flows into the cockpit," Viola called through the window.

Owen and Travis studied the labels on the switches and valves on the control panel.

"Here," Travis said, flipping a switch. There was a soft hissing noise.

Viola held the wrinkled operator's manual close to her glasses and read, "You are now ready to experience an amazing underwater world, safe inside your Water Wonder 4000."

"Okay, on the count of three," Owen said as he gripped one end of the water pipe. "One, two, three."

He and Viola lifted the pipe out of the ditch and made their way along the side of the road toward the train tracks.

"Hurry up," he snapped at Viola. If anyone saw them taking these pipes, they'd be in big trouble.

Travis and Stumpy huffed and puffed as they struggled with a pipe ahead of them.

They had all decided that four pipes should be enough to roll the submarine down to the pond.

When they turned off the main road and entered the woods, Viola whined, "Stop, Owen. I've got to rest."

Viola was so aggravating.

But Owen was trying to be patient.

Because no matter how many times he read the operator's manual, Owen was never going to understand half the stuff that Viola knew about submarines. He had let her read the manual, and she had tried and tried to explain things to him and Travis and Stumpy. But they had stared at her with openmouthed confusion until she just flapped her hand at them and said, "Oh, never mind."

By the time they finally got the last water pipe down to the submarine, Travis and Stumpy were checking the knots in the ropes they had tied to the stubby wings on both sides of the Water Wonder 4000.

They had played Rock, Paper, Scissors to see who would pull the ropes and who would move the pipes.

Owen and Stumpy would pull the ropes.

Travis and Viola would move the pipes.

"There!" Owen said, dropping his end of the pipe and lining it up with the others. He wiped his hands on his shorts. "Now how do we get the pipes under the sub?"

"Easy," Viola said. "Y'all push down on the back end and make the front end go up. Then I'll roll the pipes up under it."

TWENTY-FIVE

On the count of three," Owen said.

His heart pounded in his ears and his hands shook as he placed them against the back of the submarine.

"One."

"Two."

"Three!"

Owen and Travis and Stumpy and Viola pushed the submarine into the pond.

It glided into the water with barely a splash.

Owen and Travis scrambled to grab the ropes so the submarine wouldn't float out into the middle. Then they all four stood on the bank of the pond in silence.

They had done it!

The little red submarine was floating in Graham

Pond, bobbing in the water, sending out ripples across the surface.

"Let's tie it to the pier," Owen said.

He and Travis tied the ropes to the pier while Viola and Stumpy watched. Then Viola whipped the wrinkled, rolled-up operator's manual out of her back pocket and said, "Okay, y'all promised."

Owen groaned.

Travis rolled his eyes.

Stumpy said, "Aw, shoot."

"Y'all promised," Viola repeated.

The boys had promised Viola that before they tried to take the submarine for a ride in the pond, they would go to the hayloft for a submarine lesson. She had nagged and nagged and nagged them about how they couldn't just climb in that thing and take off.

How they needed to understand how a submarine works.

How safety was the most important thing.

And how if they didn't agree to have a submarine lesson, she might just have to remove herself from the project and let somebody with a brain (like maybe Earlene) know what was going on.

So the boys had agreed.

With one last glance over his shoulder at the Water Wonder 4000 floating in Graham Pond, Owen followed the others up the path to the barn.

Ahem. Viola cleared her throat, adjusted her glasses, and began to read from the operator's manual. "The basic principle of the ambient-pressure submersible is the same as a diving bell," she read. "It's like taking a giant drinking cup and turning it upside down and pushing it underwater. The air trapped inside stays there as long as you don't tip it too far sideways. The bottom is open to the water, so the internal pressure and external pressure are always equal."

She paused and looked at the boys over the top of the manual. "Get it?" she said.

Owen looked at Travis and Travis looked at Stumpy and Stumpy looked at Owen.

"That's why there's no hatch for an opening," Viola said. "You have to go under the water and crawl up into it. There will be air trapped inside so you can breathe."

"So all you have to do to get out is just *swim* out, right?" Stumpy said.

"Right."

Viola went on and on with the submarine lesson, pausing every now and then to sniff and sneeze. She explained how the scuba tanks would provide fresh air inside the sub. She explained how the dials and switches on the control panel kept the sub steady. She read to them the information about how there were tanks in the sub that would be flooded with water so the sub could go down.

"That's called ballast," she said.

Then she explained how the ballast tanks would be filled with air, pushing the water out so the sub could rise back up to the surface.

But the boys just looked at her.

Finally she showed them a picture of the joystick, pointing out how it was used to make the sub go up and down and forward and back.

Owen's insides danced with excitement.

"Let's go!" he hollered, hurrying to the ladder of the hayloft.

But before he had reached the floor of the barn, someone appeared in the doorway, casting a long, dark shadow over the wheelbarrow and tools and tractor parts.

Earlene.

"What are y'all doing in here?" she snapped.

Owen stepped down off the ladder and looked up at the others in the hayloft.

"Nothing," he said.

Then they all stood still as statues while Earlene ranted and raved about rotten floorboards and rats and sharp tools and all the other life-threatening dangers in the barn.

"Now get on out of here," she said, pointing toward the barn door. "And Owen Jester," she added, "you need to get in the house and visit your grandfather."

"And so I let him go," Owen told his grandfather. "Travis and Stumpy got real mad at me, but I didn't even care."

His grandfather nodded.

"Besides," Owen said, "that Frog Town idea was dumb."

Owen thought his grandfather looked better today. His face wasn't as pale and his eyes weren't as dull. He sat propped up against the pillows, studying Owen's face while Owen told him about letting Tooley go.

"I bet he's happy as anything now," Owen said. "I

bet he's swimming all around the pond, eating bugs and playing with the other frogs."

Owen looked out the window. Dark clouds had begun to roll in.

Good, he thought. It was going to rain.

Travis, Stumpy, and Viola had promised they wouldn't get in the submarine without him, but Owen still worried that they just might do it anyway. Travis, especially, could be sneaky like that. But if it rained, they probably wouldn't. They would have to wait until tomorrow, like they had promised.

Owen sat by the bed, waiting for tomorrow and listening to the sounds in the room.

His grandfather's raspy breathing.

The *tick, tick, tick* of the clock on the dresser.

The soft patter of rain on the roof.

And the *r-u-u-m-m-m* of a bullfrog down in the pond.

TWENTY-SIX

N o way!" Owen yelled.

There was no way he was going to agree to play Rock, Paper, Scissors to see who got to go in the submarine first.

He had been the one who had heard the thud.

The crack of wood.

The tumble, tumble, tumble sound.

He had been the one who had found the submarine.

So *he* was going to be the first one to drive the Water Wonder 4000.

Travis put up a good fight, arguing and cussing and hurling rocks into the pond, but finally he agreed.

"Then we'll do Rock, Paper, Scissors to see who goes with you," he said.

But Owen shook his head. "No way," he said again.

Travis glared at him. "Who made you boss of the world?" he said.

"Yeah," Stumpy said. "Who made you boss of the world?"

Viola sneezed.

Owen hesitated. He knew that what he was about to say was risky. He was setting himself up to be teased for the rest of his life.

But he took a deep breath and said it.

"Viola should be the one to go."

Travis's mouth dropped open. Stumpy's eyes widened. Viola grinned.

Now that he had said it, Owen was ready to throw caution to the wind and just get it all out.

"Look," he said. "*She's* the one who figured out how to get that sub down here to the pond."

Viola blushed.

"And *she's* the one who figured out that stuff about ambient pressure and ballast and all," Owen continued. "Viola should be the one to go with me."

"Okay then," Travis said. "Let's see Miss Know-It-All get in that water." He whirled around and jabbed a finger at Viola. "I hope a water moccasin don't bite you," he said.

Viola's face grew instantly pale. She looked at the pond, her red-rimmed, watery eyes wide with worry. Then she tossed her hair back, lifted her chin, and said, "Shut up, Travis."

So Owen and Viola waded into the pond. The water was warm. The bottom squishy with mud.

Owen swam out to the submarine tied to the end of the dock. Then he took a deep breath, ducked under the water, and crawled into the opening in the bottom of the sub. When he came up out of the water, he was inside the little compartment, looking out of the bubble-shaped window at Travis and Stumpy standing on the dock. Just as he settled into one of the little seats, Viola appeared beside him, sputtering and gasping and pushing at her glasses. She brushed a soggy leaf off her blue-striped bathing suit and climbed up into the seat next to Owen.

Owen beamed at Viola.

Viola beamed at Owen.

There they were beaming at each other again and Owen didn't even care if Travis and Stumpy saw them.

"Okay," he said. "Let's do it." He looked out the window and gave Travis and Stumpy the signal to untie the rope from the dock.

Viola took the operator's manual out of the plastic sandwich bag she had tucked into the strap of her bathing suit. She flipped to the page with the heading

READY, SET, GO:
Starting Your Water Wonder 4000

As Viola read, Owen flipped the switches.

"Now open the forward and aft flood valves," Viola read.

"Here goes," Owen said. He turned the valves and heard the *whoosh* of water inside the tanks and the *blurb, blurb, blurb* of bubbles outside the window.

"Now push down on the thumb switch on top of the joystick," Viola said.

Owen's heart raced and his hands trembled.

He counted to three.

One.

Two.

Three.

The little propellers on the stubby wings began to spin . . .

. . . and the Water Wonder 4000 went down . . .

. . . down . . .

. . . down . . .

. . . under the water in Graham Pond.

CHAPTER
TWENTY-SEVEN

Owen had to admit that when they first sank below the surface of the pond, his stomach did a major somersault and he considered for a blip of a millisecond scrambling through the opening in the bottom of the sub and getting the heck out of there.

But once that blip of a millisecond passed, his somersaulting stomach settled down and he was able to take in the magnificent awesomeness of what he was doing.

He was riding in a submarine under the water in Graham Pond.

Viola pointed to the drawing in the manual to show Owen how the joystick worked to make the submarine go up and down, back and forth, left and right.

"Okay," he said. "Here goes."

He pushed the joystick forward, and the little submarine began to move.

Slowly, slowly, slowly away from the dock and out into the middle of the pond.

All Owen could see out of the windows was the murky water. But gradually, his eyes began to adjust and he could see more clearly. He saw little silver minnows darting through the water.

He saw turtles. The same shiny black turtles that he used to see sunning on logs on hot afternoons.

He saw a rotten tree stump and a rusty soda can.

A fishing lure, an old shoe, a broken bottle.

And then . . .

. . . he saw a frog!

A bullfrog.

A big, green bullfrog.

But it wasn't Tooley.

He knew it wasn't Tooley because it didn't have the heart-shaped red spot between its eyes.

Owen had been so absorbed in the magnificent awesomeness of the submarine ride that he had forgotten all about Viola sitting next to him until she said, "Let's look for that frog of yours."

Of course!

That's what they would do!

They would ride around Graham Pond and look for Tooley.

So that's what they did.

At first, Owen wasn't very good at maneuvering the Water Wonder 4000 around the pond. But before long, he got the hang of it. He was able to move the little submarine forward and back. He could turn it right and turn it left.

So he and Viola looked for frogs.

"There's one!"

"There's another one!"

But none of them were Tooley.

Until . . .

"There he is!" Owen shouted.

Sure enough, swimming along outside the bubble-shaped window was the biggest, greenest, slimiest, most beautiful bullfrog ever to be seen in Carter, Georgia . . .

. . . with a heart-shaped red spot between its bulging yellow eyes.

Owen guided the submarine along beside Tooley.

He put his hand on the window.

Tooley stopped swimming and bumped his nose against the glass.

Owen looked right into those bulging froggy eyes and he knew . . .

. . . that frog was happy.

"We better head back," Viola said.

They had read in the operator's manual that the air supply of the Water Wonder 4000 was only good for about two hours. The air supply gauge on the control panel was almost at the halfway mark. They had better head back so Travis and Stumpy could have a turn.

Owen had some trouble maneuvering the submarine close to the dock without crashing into it, but eventually, he got close enough. Using the joystick, Owen brought the submarine up toward the surface of the water.

"Turn on the forward and aft blow valves," Viola read from the manual.

Owen turned the valves. There was a hissing sound as air filled the tanks, forcing the water out.

The little submarine began to rise slowly up out of the pond.

They had done it! They had taken the Water Wonder 4000 for a ride in Graham Pond!

But then . . .

. . . Owen looked out the front window and felt a blanket of doom settle over him.

There on the dock was a cluster of frantic-looking grownups, waving and yelling and gesturing, with Travis and Stumpy standing droopy-faced and slump-shouldered beside them.

TWENTY-EIGHT

Owen's father had been furious.

His mother had been livid.

Earlene had been outraged.

And the three men from the railroad company had been all of those things but mostly relieved to see the Water Wonder 4000 safe and sound and floating in the pond. They had been looking for it for a long time. When they had finally found the splintered wooden crate beside the train tracks and seen the trees and bushes cleared all the way to the pond, they had put two and two together.

Now Owen was sitting in his bedroom, where he was going to have to stay for one whole week.

He hadn't been allowed to go down to the pond to watch the flatbed tow truck pull the Water Wonder

4000 out of the pond and drive up the side of the tracks to take the submarine away.

Travis and Stumpy and Viola hadn't been allowed to go either.

He hadn't been allowed to go down to the dock when his father had dismantled the perfect frog cage and tossed it into the junk heap behind the shed.

Travis and Stumpy and Viola hadn't been allowed to go either.

Owen stared glumly out of his bedroom window and watched Pete and Leroy romping in the yard below.

He let out a big, heaving sigh.

The telephone rang.

Earlene marched down the hallway, her heavy shoes making a *clomp, clomp* noise on the wooden floor that echoed up the stairs.

Owen tiptoed to his bedroom door to listen.

Earlene answered the phone.

"Hello?"

Pause.

"Owen *Jester*?"

Owen opened the door a crack and stood still and quiet.

"Who is this?" Earlene snapped.

Pause.

"Well . . . he . . . yes . . . just a minute."

Earlene clomped up the stairs, and Owen scurried over to his bed, pretending to read his book of Bible stories.

Earlene pushed the bedroom door open and thrust the phone toward Owen. "Some man is on the phone for you."

Owen set the book aside. "Who?"

Earlene's mouth was set in that harsh way of hers. "Some man from that submarine company."

Water Wonder Technologies?

Owen's heart raced.

As if he hadn't gotten into enough trouble already, now that submarine guy was probably mad as all get-out. He was probably going to yell at Owen. Maybe he was going to call the police. Maybe he had *already* called the police. Maybe Owen would have to go to jail.

Owen didn't feel too good.

Earlene shook the phone at him.

Owen's hand trembled a little as he reached to take it.

"Hello?" His voice came out kind of wobbly.

Owen listened.

And then his heavy heart lightened and his worried stomach settled.

This man wasn't mad.

This man wanted to shake his hand!

This man thought it was wonderful that Owen and Viola had managed to take the Water Wonder 4000 down under the water in Graham Pond and drive around and look at frogs and turtles and come back up to the surface and right on over to the dock, where all those angry folks had been waiting for them.

This man wanted to come to Owen's house and meet him and Viola and even Travis and Stumpy.

After Owen hung up, he raced past grumpy old Earlene and ran downstairs to tell his parents.

"He's the *owner* of Water Wonder Technologies!" Owen said, beaming at his father.

"He's coming all the way from Canada to meet me." Owen grinned at his mother.

"Can I go tell Viola?" Owen hopped from one foot to the other.

Please. Please. Please.

He could feel Earlene's disapproving glare be-hind him.

His father chuckled and flapped his hand. "Aw, go on," he said. "But come right back."

Owen was out the door before Earlene could blink.

CHAPTER
TWENTY-NINE

Owen and Travis and Stumpy and Viola sat on Owen's front porch and stared up the road.

Waiting.

Waiting.

Waiting.

Owen had been allowed out of the house for one day and one day only. But what a day it was going to be!

That man from Water Wonder Technologies would be arriving any minute.

His name was Ron.

He was bringing a reporter from the Macon *Telegraph* to interview them.

They were going to tell the reporter how Owen had found the submarine and how they had cleared the way to the pond. They were going to explain how they had used water pipes the way the Egyptians had used logs to move the stones when they built the pyramids. (And Owen would be sure to tell the reporter that they had taken the water pipes back to Sycamore Road. But he would probably leave out the part about how much his father had hollered at him about those pipes.)

After a little arguing, Owen and Travis and Stumpy had agreed that they would tell the reporter that Viola was the one who figured out how to drive the submarine.

And *then*, they were all going over to the railroad freight yard to have their picture taken with the Water Wonder 4000.

Owen raced up the stairs, waving the newspaper. He burst into his grandfather's room and hurried over to the bed.

"Look!" He held the paper in front of his grandfather and jabbed a finger at the photograph.

There he was, Owen Jester, standing stiff and proud beside the Water Wonder 4000, his hand resting on the bubble-shaped window.

Viola posed on the other side of the submarine, grinning, her eyes looking big and wide through her thick glasses. Travis and Stumpy stood slightly behind her, Stumpy making a peace sign and Travis looking a little irritated to be standing in the back.

Printed in big bold letters above the photograph was the headline

CHILDREN TOUR LOCAL POND IN SUBMARINE

Beside the photograph was an article all about Owen and Viola (and a little bit about Travis and Stumpy).

Owen read the article to his grandfather—the whole story, right there in the Macon *Telegraph* . . .

Starting with the night Owen had heard the thud.

The crack of wood.

The tumble, tumble, tumble sound . . .

And ending when he and Viola had maneuvered the little submarine through the murky water of Graham Pond and then had managed to get safely back up to the surface.

"A spokesman for the railroad reported that the Water Wonder 4000 is once again on its way to the Sun and Sand Tropical Resort in Miami, Florida," Owen read.

He folded the newspaper and grinned at his grand-father. He felt a little guilty that he hadn't told him about the submarine when he had first found it. Owen hoped his grandfather wouldn't be mad that he had kept such a fantastic secret from him.

Owen's grandfather lifted a hand off the bed and gave Owen a shaky thumbs-up.

CHAPTER
THIRTY

When his week of punishment was finally over, Owen raced downstairs and burst through the screen door with Earlene hollering after him about staying away from the hayloft and the train tracks and the pond.

Owen went straight down to the pond and sat on the dock. The morning sun felt warm on his arms. A dragonfly flitted around in front of him and then settled on the dock beside him. Owen rested his chin on his knees and waited.

And waited.

And waited.

Each time he saw a bullfrog poke its head out of the water or climb onto a log, Owen didn't move a muscle. He squinted over at the frog to look for the heart-shaped red spot.

Finally . . .

. . . it happened.

A green frog head poked up through a cluster of rotting oak leaves near the edge of the pond.

And right between the bulging yellow eyes was a heart-shaped red spot.

Owen's insides flipped with excitement.

He lifted his chin slowly, slowly, slowly off his knees so he could get a better look.

Yep.

That was a heart-shaped red spot, all right.

The frog swam lazily toward the dock and stopped, floating on the surface of the water with its long froggy legs stretched out behind it.

That frog was happy.

Owen was sure of it.

That frog didn't want to live in a perfect cage.

That frog didn't want to be mayor of Frog Town.

That frog didn't want to be Tooley Graham.

The short, sad life of Tooley Graham was over.

That night, Owen sat by the window and took a deep breath of the summer night air. It smelled like pine and grass and honeysuckle.

Far off in the distance, the train whistle blew. Owen waited, listening for the faint clatter of the train on the tracks to get louder and louder as it got closer to Carter.

In a blink, the train was whooshing down the tracks behind the house.

Clatter, clatter, clatter.

Then the *clatter, clatter, clatter* grew fainter and fainter until the only sound left was the chirp of the crickets in the garden beneath the window . . .

. . . and the *r-u-u-u-m-m-m* of the bullfrogs down in the pond.

GOFISH

QUESTIONS FOR THE AUTHOR

BARBARA O'CONNOR

Grady O'Connor

What did you want to be when you grew up?
For most of my childhood, I wanted to be a teacher. I also thought I might like to be a dance instructor and have my own dancing school, which I actually did for a few years.

When did you realize you wanted to be a writer?
I don't remember ever making a conscious decision to be a writer. Writing was just something that I loved doing from a very young age. I still have boxes and boxes of things I wrote as a child, from poems to stories to plays.

What's your most embarrassing childhood memory?
I was one of those kids who was always picked last for a team. (I'm terrible at sports.) I always hated that.

What's your favorite childhood memory?
Summer camp. Loved it. The woods. The cabins. The Smoky Mountains.

As a young person, who did you look up to most?
My dad.

What was your favorite thing about school?
I loved anything organized, like worksheets and schedules and charts.

What was your least favorite thing about school?
Having to be quiet. A teacher once reprimanded me for being "loquacious." When I asked her what that meant, of course she told me to look it up. I have never forgotten the meaning of that word!

What were your hobbies as a kid? What are your hobbies now?
I loved collecting things, like stamps and bottle caps. I enjoyed tap dancing and writing. I still enjoy tap dancing and writing. I also like to garden and walk with my dogs.

What was your first job, and what was your "worst" job?
I used to teach dancing lessons to neighborhood children. I had a dance studio in my garage that my father helped me make.

My worst job was selling pots and pans door-to-door. As a bonus for buying the pots and pans, the buyer would receive a free set of china. I was supposed to turn the teacup upside down and stand on it to show how sturdy it was. I never did. I also never sold any pots and pans.

How did you celebrate publishing your first book?
With lots of whooping and yahoo-ing—and then dinner out with my family.

Where do you write your books?
In the winter, I write in my office, which is a converted bedroom in my house. I have a huge, lovely desk that was handmade by

a friend of mine. The wood is beautiful and there is lots of room for family photos. My two dogs always stay in there with me and keep me company.

In the summer, I love to sit out on my screened-in porch. I love being able to watch the birds and look at the flowers while I write.

What sparked your imagination for *The Fantastic Secret of Owen Jester*?

When I was in the third grade, I lived in Louisiana. There was a drainage ditch that ran in front of my house. An enormous bullfrog lived in the water in that ditch. I was determined to catch him, but the slightest movement would send him swimming up inside the drainage pipe that ran under the driveway. So I rigged up a trap using a birdcage. I actually caught him! I kept him in a giant tub for a few days and then put him back in the ditch, where I knew he belonged. He was just like Tooley Graham!

Of the books you've written, which is your favorite?

Greetings from Nowhere. I enjoyed writing the multiple viewpoints.

What challenges do you face in the writing process, and how do you overcome them?

It's always a challenge to stay true to my writing voice so that it sounds unique but natural. I overcome that by staying focused and not forcing the writing. I try to let it flow naturally. Plotting is always a challenge, too. I overcome that by lots of hard work: outlining as I go along, taking the story into new directions, experimenting, having trusted readers to critique the story, and reading other books.

Which of your characters is most like you?

Jennalee in *Me and Rupert Goody.* I think I felt the most like her as I wrote her story and I definitely related to the setting of the Smoky Mountains, where I spent a lot of time as a child.

What makes you laugh out loud?

Kids and dogs.

What do you do on a rainy day?

I like to read and write. Love crossword puzzles and playing Scrabble online.

What's your idea of fun?

I love to walk with my dogs. That probably doesn't sound like much fun, but it is! I live near cranberry bogs and it's a great place to walk. There is a lot of wildlife there. Today I saw a fox and a pair of swans.

What's your favorite song?

I love country-and-western music. I love gospel music. I love show tunes. All kinds of music.

Who is your favorite fictional character?

Beverly Cleary's Ramona Quimby.

What was your favorite book when you were a kid? Do you have a favorite book now?

I loved *The Pink Motel* by Carol Ryrie Brinks. I also read all the Trixie Belden and Nancy Drew mysteries.

Two of my favorite books now are *The Liar's Club* by Mary Karr and *Don't Let's Go to the Dogs Tonight* by Alexandra Fuller.

What's your favorite TV show or movie?
Judge Judy.

If you were stranded on a desert island, who would you want for company?
Probably somebody who was very good at building boats out of things you find on a desert island.

If you could travel anywhere in the world, where would you go and what would you do?
I love Ireland and would like to go back there. I would just drive around the countryside and enjoy the people and the beauty.

If you could travel in time, where would you go and what would you do?
The fifties. Everything seemed much simpler then. (But I would miss the Internet.)

What's the best advice you have ever received about writing?
Author Linda Sue Park often passes down advice that she got from Katherine Paterson, which is to set a goal of writing two pages a day. That doesn't seem nearly as daunting as sitting down to write a novel.

Do you ever get writer's block? What do you do to get back on track?
I sure do! Taking a long walk and thinking about it helps. I also sometimes ask myself, "What if?" That often takes the story in a new direction.

Having a friend who is a writer helps a lot, too. She reads my work and helps me see where the manuscript needs work and lets me bounce ideas off of her.

What do you want readers to remember about your books?
The characters. I also hope they had fun reading them.

What would you do if you ever stopped writing?
I'd love to be a librarian, but it's probably too late, since I'd have to go back to school and I'm not sure I'm ready for that anymore. So, I guess I'd just stay home and play with my dogs and work in my garden and figure out a way to pay the electric bill.

What do you like best about yourself?
I'm very organized and always punctual. I also think I have a pretty good sense of humor. I'm also very good at keeping secrets.

Do you have any strange or funny habits? Did you when you were a kid?
I'm always too early. (I spend a lot of time waiting on people but no one ever has to wait on me.) I was like that as a kid, too.

What do you consider to be your greatest accomplishment?
My greatest accomplishment is having raised a good son who is honest and kind. But I'm also pretty proud of having written books.

What do you wish you could do better?
I wish I could sing and draw better. And I wish I could play a musical instrument.

What would your readers be most surprised to learn about you?
I have no sense of smell and I can eat a whole bag of goldfish crackers.

Popeye doesn't think anything exciting will ever happen in Fayette, South Carolina. That is, until Elvis arrives and tiny paper boats carrying handwritten notes float one by one down the creek . . .

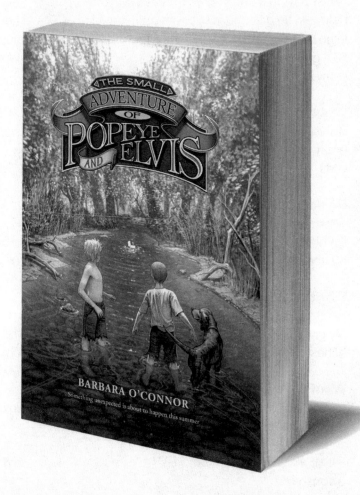

Can the boys solve the mystery of the secret messages?
Find out in *The Small Adventure of Popeye and Elvis*
by BARBARA O'CONNOR

1

DRIP.

Drip.

Drip.

Popeye opened his eye and looked up at the heart-shaped stain on the ceiling of his bedroom. Rusty water squeezed out of the hole in the peeling plaster and dropped onto the foot of his bed.

Drip.

Drip.

Drip.

It had been raining for over a week.

All day.

Every day.

The stain on the ceiling used to be a tiny circle. Popeye had watched it grow a little more each day.

He got out of bed and nudged Boo with his foot. The old dog lifted his head and looked up at Popeye, his sagging skin drooping down over his sad, watery eyes.

"Still raining," Popeye said.

Boo's big, heavy head flopped back down on the floor, and he let out a long, low dog groan.

Popeye padded across the cracked linoleum floor of the hallway and into the bathroom. He splashed water on his face and ran his wet fingers over his head. The stubble of his new summer buzz cut felt scratchy, like a cat's tongue. His white scalp showed through his pale blond hair.

He examined his teeth in the mirror.

They looked clean.

He rubbed his good eye.

Then he rubbed his bad eye. The one that was always squinted shut thanks to his uncle Dooley.

Popeye hadn't always been Popeye. Before he was three years old, he had been Henry.

But when he was three, his uncle Dooley had

placed a small green crab apple on the fence post out back and turned to his girlfriend and said, "Watch this, Charlene."

Then he had walked back twenty paces, like a gunslinger, taken aim with his Red Ryder BB gun, and pulled the trigger.

Dooley was not a very good aim.

Charlene was not impressed.

When the BB hit Henry square in the eye, she had screamed bloody murder and carried on so much that when Popeye's grandmother, Velma, came running out of the house to see what all the fuss was about, she had thought it was Charlene who'd been shot in the eye.

Popeye had been Popeye ever since.

And Charlene was long gone. (Which hadn't bothered Dooley one little bit 'cause there were plenty more where she came from.)

Popeye went up the hall to the kitchen, his bare feet stirring up little puffs of dust on the floor. Velma didn't care much about keeping a clean house. She mainly cared about not cracking up.

"You get old, you crack up," she told Popeye

when she couldn't find her reading glasses or opened the closet door and forgot why.

While Popeye made toast with powdered sugar on top, Velma sat at the kitchen table with her eyes closed, reciting the kings and queens of England in chronological order.

"Edward V, Richard III, Henry VII, Henry VIII, Edward VI, Mary I . . ."

Popeye knew that when she got to the last one, Elizabeth II, she would probably start all over again.

"Egbert, Ethelwulf, Ethelbald, Ethelbert . . ."

Reciting the kings and queens of England in chronological order was exercising Velma's brain and keeping her from cracking up.

But sometimes, Popeye worried that it wasn't working.

This was a big worry.

Popeye needed Velma to not crack up because no one else in his family was very good at taking care of things.

Not his father, who lived up in Chattanooga and sold smoke-damaged rugs out of the back of a pickup truck.

Not his mother, who came and went but never

told anybody where she came from or where she went to.

And definitely not his uncle Dooley, who lived in a rusty trailer in the backyard and sometimes worked at the meatpacking plant and sometimes sold aluminum siding and sometimes watched TV all day.

Popeye's grandmother, Velma, was the only one good at taking care of things.

"Edward VIII, George VI, Elizabeth II." Velma opened her eyes. Instead of starting all over again with Egbert, she shuffled over to the kitchen counter and poured herself a cup of coffee.

"Hey there, burrhead," she said, running her hand over Popeye's fuzzy buzz cut.

"Hey."

"What're you gonna do today?"

Popeye shrugged.

"This dern rain is driving me nuts," she said, stirring a heaping spoonful of sugar into her coffee.

Popeye stared out at the muddy yard. A waterfall of rust-colored rainwater poured off the edge of the metal roof of the shed out back and made a river. The river snaked its way down the gravel driveway and into the drainage ditch that ran along the side of the road. The ditch was nearly overflowing. Every now and then, soda cans or plastic bags floated by in front of the house.

Boo ambled into the kitchen and ate a scrap of toast off the floor under the table, his tail wagging in slow motion.

Back . . .

And forth.

Back . . .

And forth.

Popeye licked powdered sugar off his fingers and went into the living room.

Dooley was stretched out on the couch, snoring one of those throat-gurgling kinds of snores. The smell of cigarettes hovered in the air around him and clung to the worn corduroy couch.

Popeye flopped into Velma's big armchair. The metal tray table beside it was stacked with crossword puzzle magazines. Crossword puzzles were good brain exercises, too. Velma knew more words than anybody. She taught Popeye one new word every week. He wrote it on the patio with sidewalk chalk and studied it until it got smudged up by Dooley's worn-out work boots or washed away by the rain.

This week's word was *vicissitude*, but he hadn't been able to write it on the patio yet because of the rain.

vicissitude: *noun*; a change of circumstances, typically one that is unwelcome or unpleasant

Popeye slouched down in the chair and slapped his bare foot on the floor.

Slap.

Slap.

He looked out the window, wishing that maybe some vicissitude would come along and make this dern rain stop. Even something unwelcome or unpleasant would probably be better than this.

He watched a fly land on Dooley's big toe.

He wrote *vicissitude* with his finger on the flowered fabric of Velma's chair.

He scooped saltine cracker crumbs off the coffee table and tossed them over to Boo, who had settled onto his raggedy quilt by the woodstove.

The hands of the clock over the couch jerked noisily.

Tick. Tick. Tick.

Around and around.

Tick. Tick. Tick.

Popeye was beginning to hate that clock. He was sick to high heaven of watching it turn minutes into hours and hours into days.

Every day the same.

So *what* if the rain stopped? Popeye thought.

It would still be boring.

It would always be boring in Fayette, South Carolina.

Every day would always be the same.

Popeye was certain about that.

But Popeye was wrong.

Because that very day, that day with the rain dripping out of the heart-shaped stain on the ceiling and that fly sitting there on Dooley's big toe, things changed.

Elvis came to town.